Grave Inheritance

Rachael O. Phillips

Annie's®

AnniesFiction.com

Library of Congress-in-Publication Data
Grave Inheritance/ by Rachael O. Phillips
p. cm.
I. Title
                    2016962979

AnniesFiction.com
(800) 282-6643
Amish Inn Mysteries™
Series Creator: Shari Lohner
Series Editor: Jane Haertel
Cover Illustrator: Kelley McMorris

10 11 12 13 14 | Printed in China | 9 8 7 6 5 4 3 2 1

1

"Cyrus Whittington?" Sadie Schwarzentruber, Liz Eckardt's friend and tenant, stared over Liz's shoulder at her old-fashioned guest register. "Mondays are boring enough around here. But he sounds like some old guy who wears slippers all day and alphabetizes his liniments." She snorted. "Why can't somebody interesting stay at your bed-and-breakfast this week?"

Liz, the owner of the Olde Mansion Inn, crossed her arms, but couldn't help grinning. "I could invite Emily Hart back. She was the most interesting 'librarian' I've ever met. Or should I say Jennifer? Regardless, she might like a change of scenery." Emily Hart, whose real name was Jennifer Clayton, had been one of Liz's first guests, and had committed a number of crimes, including murdering a fellow guest and kidnapping one of Liz's employees.

Sadie rolled her eyes.

Mary Ann Berne, Sadie's business partner, said, "I hope they keep her in jail for a hundred years."

Liz shuddered. "Fortunately, guests like her are few and far between." Shaking off the memory, Liz gladly recalled her conversation with Mr. Whittington. "Cyrus sounded interesting on the phone—spoke with just a touch of a British accent. Sort of like Cary Grant."

"I *love* Cary Grant movies," Sadie cooed.

Even Mary Ann, often too busy to entertain romantic notions, twirled a lock of her shoulder-length silver bob. Within seconds, though, she'd assumed what Liz privately called her "Queen Mary Ann" expression. "Save it for popcorn night, Sadie. It's already August, and we've got planning to do. Lots of fall fabrics to unpack."

"Relax, Mary Ann. Sew Welcome won't fall apart if we hang out here in the rotunda a few minutes." She cocked her head at Liz. "Maybe until Mr. Whittington shows up?"

Liz countered, "He won't arrive for an hour. Why don't you come for coffee and snacks? I'll introduce him then."

"We'll both come," Mary Ann said. She shot a pointed glance at Sadie. "*If* we get all our boxes unpacked."

"See you at four," Sadie called as Mary Ann steered her toward their shop.

Liz listened to the partners' banter as they disappeared into Sew Welcome. She couldn't imagine life without Sadie and Mary Ann. Yet Liz had moved to Pleasant Creek, Indiana, from Boston not that long ago. Who could have known that they, along with the other Material Girls—their quilting group—would become her best friends?

Even as Liz grappled with the inn's budget on her laptop, she basked in the knowledge that this elegant old mansion belonged to her. She could have worked mostly uninterrupted in her own quarters or in the library. But she sometimes liked this small reception desk in the rotunda, whose high ceiling and magnificent stairway gave her a heady sense of spaciousness. This summer, Liz had displayed some of the Material Girls' bright-colored quilts on racks throughout the rotunda. But her favorite, by far, was the baby quilt sewn by her Amish great-grandmother. Liz's late mother had willed it to her, a clue that had led Liz to Indiana and her Amish relatives. Her cousin Miriam, Aunt Ruth, and Uncle Amos had helped fill the emptiness left after her mother died and her godson, Steve—whom she'd raised as her own—left for military service overseas.

A snore interrupted her musings. Beans, the English bulldog, flopped on his—and Liz's—favorite rug near the foyer's front entry.

He'd lain there the better part of each day ever since Liz unknowingly had purchased him, along with the inn. Beans looked unspeakably comfortable.

If only she had a squirt bottle.

But knowing Beans, even that might not elicit more than a half-raised eyelid.

"It's not fair," Liz declared, though she knelt and checked to see if he was breathing. Reassured, she shook a finger at him. "I do the work around here, but you take all the naps. Someday, I'll invite a whole Cub Scout troop to zap you with water guns."

Beans didn't flick an ear.

He knew perfectly well Liz would never carry out her dastardly promise. Even a hundred armed and dangerous Cub Scouts would stand no chance against Beans, for Sadie adored the air he breathed and would protect him.

"I say, would you really interrupt the dear old fellow's nap?" The British-sounding male voice above Liz held the promise of a smile. "A rude awakening indeed."

Liz leaned back on her heels and hoped her surprise didn't show. A worn black top hat crowned the man's elderly, aristocratic face. She found her voice. "I wouldn't think of it. But don't tell Beans."

"Beans? A unique name." He lowered his voice to a conspiratorial whisper. "We'll keep your *terrible* threat our little secret."

Chuckling, Liz stood. "Mr. Cyrus Whittington?"

The white-haired man touched his hat brim. "The same. And do I have the pleasure of addressing Ms. Liz Eckardt?"

"Yes. The pleasure is mine." The man's accent and hat, plus his enormous bow tie, faded orange-and-green-checked shirt, baggy pants, and plaid flannel slippers, were quite . . . unusual. By the time she'd registered him, given him the key to the Somewhere in Time Room, and described the inn's amenities, she was speaking BBC too. And what an entry his photo would make in her guest album.

He seemed delighted at the prospect of coffee hour. Liz hid a grin as she anticipated Sadie's reaction. *Mr. Whittington's wearing slippers, but I don't think he's quite what you expected.*

He'd listed a Fort Wayne address, which puzzled her. Perhaps he'd emigrated from Great Britain. But why would he stay in a B&B less than a hundred miles away from Fort Wayne?

No sooner had Mr. Whittington made his way upstairs than Tony Lanham appeared.

Liz had almost forgotten that another guest was coming today. Mr. Lanham was a stocky, fuzzy-haired businessman who was attending an appliance sales conference in a nearby town. As she handed him the key to the Sunset Room, he enthused, "I'm glad the hotels were filled up there. I like small towns and big old houses."

"Me too. I love Pleasant Creek." She chatted about her own move from Boston, mentally categorizing Mr. Lanham as an easy guest.

He was personable, though his smiles often seemed like apologies. After meeting Mr. Whittington, Tony seemed so very ordinary in his navy golf shirt and khakis.

A sudden movement by Beans's rug made Liz blink. Was she seeing things?

Beans had sat up. Without the *whirrrr* of a can opener that promised him dinner. Without any offer of a treat. He gazed adoringly at Tony as the businessman murmured, "You're a fine fella, aren't you?" and unerringly found the bulldog's favorite scratching spots.

Liz introduced the two, but Tony needed no introduction as far as Beans was concerned. Liz saw no difference between the man's treatment and any other dog-loving guest's. But Beans's big mouth had widened in a huge doggy smile, as if he'd known Tony all his life.

What was going on? Beans accepted other guests' attentions as his due, but mostly, he preferred uninterrupted naps. Nor was he acting aggressively, as he did when he smelled one of his favorite treats, peanut butter, on guests.

Instead, he groaned in ecstasy as Tony scratched his belly, grinning as if he'd met his soul mate.

Liz felt rather than saw Sadie's gaze behind her. Liz turned, but Sadie already had scooted beside Beans's rug, wearing an overly polite expression Liz did not trust.

"My, Beans really seems to like you." Sadie spoke through a fake smile.

"He's an awesome dog." Tony chuckled as Beans nosed his hand for more.

Quickly Liz introduced them.

"Call me Tony." He beamed.

Sadie didn't. "Nice to meet you, Mr. Lanham."

Liz winced.

Sadie continued, "Liz might have forgotten to mention that Beans gets sick easily. I had to take him to the vet this past month because he just wasn't himself. He really needs his afternoon nap."

"Oh. I'm sorry." Tony stood, casting a confused glance toward Liz, then Sadie.

Liz grabbed his small suitcase and steered Tony to the stairway, chattering about Pleasant Creek's downtown and summer activities. He seemed most interested in the local eatery, Mama's Home Cooking, and Sweet Everything, the bakery owned by her friend and fellow Material Girl, Naomi Mason. "Have I come to the right place or what?"

"You certainly have." Liz safely delivered Tony to the Sunset Room.

Don't be such a worrywart, Liz. Sadie might be a little jealous of Beans's preference for Tony, but he was staying only two days, and he'd be away at meetings most of the time.

———— //////////////////////////// ————

Fortunately, Sadie's interest in meeting Liz's Cary Grant voice-alike trumped her wariness of Tony, as did Mary Ann's bringing Sadie's favorite coconut cream pie for coffee hour that afternoon.

While Sadie said little to Tony, she introduced herself to Mr. Whittington with her usual friendly flair. "Are you from England? I love your accent."

"No, I am an American, but I have spent a great deal of time in England."

Mr. Whittington had seen Buckingham Palace, Shakespeare's Strand Theatre, and the Tower of London many times. He'd ridden boats on the Thames, viewed the white cliffs of Dover, and crossed the Channel to France. "Rough going, indeed. Didn't have the Chunnel then. I feared we should never arrive on the other side."

An affable, unique guest always made coffee hour a pleasure. Liz almost forgot about the pie until Sadie cast a meaningful—and eager—glance toward it. Mary Ann, grinning, rose to serve dessert.

Meanwhile, Mr. Whittington had discovered both Sadie and Mary Ann knew something about local history. "Capital! I was hoping to meet someone who knew about the early glassworks in your area. I worked in glass manufacturing for many years."

"You really should visit the stained glass factory in Kokomo," Sadie advised.

"Absolutely," Mary Ann agreed as she cut her pie. "Its owners still use much of the same equipment and processes from more than a century ago."

As Mr. Whittington regarded the dessert with great interest, Mary Ann offered him a large slice. "Would you care for a piece?"

"I certainly would."

"So would I!" Tony blurted, then reddened. "I mean, if that's all right. I don't want to intrude."

"The pie is for everyone." Mary Ann served him a huge slice. "You're not intruding at all."

Liz and Mary Ann drew Tony into the conversation. Tony even told a few fun stories himself.

"Your company actually makes a black-and-white-spotted refrigerator?" Liz asked, after Tony brought it up.

"Yes, only Apex Appliances makes a fridge like it. We call it our Chilly Cow Special." Tony laughed. "When customers open it, it moos. Love to watch the security camera recordings in that department. People jump a mile high."

He and Mr. Whittington shifted the conversation to cars, and the older man offered to show them all his vintage convertible.

As they walked to the parking lot, Liz, who owned a sleek black Acura with all the bells and whistles, thought his car might prove interesting.

At the sight of it, they all halted in their tracks.

Mr. Whittington stood beside a vintage, dark green convertible, every inch shining with Hollywood elegance, from its sleek silver hood ornament to spotless whitewalls. Liz could almost see sultry Bette Davis or debonair Clark Gable stepping from its opulent green leather interior to a red carpet welcome.

"That's the prettiest thing I've seen in fifty years," Sadie purred as she stroked the car's fender.

"Thank you." Mr. Whittington smiled broadly. "Reginald is a 1931 Auburn coupe, built right here in Indiana."

Sadie turned an eager face to the owner. "Can I look under the hood?"

He propped it open for her, and Tony joined them. A lover of all things mechanical—Sadie maintained her own farm vehicles—she enthused with the men about the car's motor in terms Liz couldn't begin to comprehend.

Meanwhile, Mary Ann seemed lost in 1930s movieland. She hadn't said a word yet—*very* unlike Mary Ann.

Liz pondered the scene. How could Mr. Whittington, with his eclectic scarecrow ensemble, fit with this gleaming aristocrat of an automobile? Yet he did.

Listening to Sadie's and Tony's homage, the owner nodded approvingly. "I *am* quite fond of the old fellow." He patted the ivory-colored steering wheel. "Reg belonged to my father, and we've traveled many miles together. Not many lately, as we both creak more than we used to. But when contractors building my home in Fort Wayne kept encountering delays, Reg and I decided to take a short road trip."

"It's beautiful," Mary Ann breathed.

His smile shone as brightly as his car's chrome. "It is a lovely day—quite warm, but perfect for a ride with the top down." Mr. Whittington opened the coupe's passenger door and bowed. "I regret that Reg and I can accommodate only one passenger at a time. But would any of you care to go for a spin?"

"We'd love to!" they chorused, though Tony said a regretful good-bye.

"Apex Appliances must be the apex of your day," he quoted—apparently the company employee motto—and left for his meetings.

Liz expected Sadie to hurdle everyone for the coveted spot.

Instead, she gestured to Mary Ann. "You first."

Her partner blinked. "Why . . . thank you."

"We shall return in perhaps a half hour?" Mr. Whittington cocked his head at Mary Ann.

She nodded and curled gracefully into the front seat, waving, then brushing a perfectly manicured hand through her hair as she and Mr. Whittington drove off.

Liz patted Sadie on the shoulder. "How nice of you."

"Yes, wasn't it?" Sadie grinned wickedly. "Go next, will you? Then maybe I can get the longest ride."

Chuckling, Liz agreed. After whipping through coffee hour cleanup, she considered changing clothes. A denim skirt and tee hardly fit the coupe's era.

Don't be silly. But the right hat would do the trick.

Months before, a guest had forgotten a big white hat, its crown encircled with a blue ribbon, à la *Easter Parade.* The guest had been indifferent to its return.

Liz anchored the hat with an antique pin she'd found recently at a flea market. Sadie was the one who usually wore extravagant head coverings, and Liz felt a trifle self-conscious. She shook it off and assumed a Judy Garland pose in front of the foyer mirror.

Not bad.

Liz walked out to the parking lot just as Reg, Mr. Whittington, and Mary Ann pulled in.

"Adorable!" Mary Ann, exiting the car, touched Liz's brim.

A surprisingly tender smile curved her chauffeur's mouth. "When I was small, my mother wore a hat like that—blue ribbon and all."

Liz took Mary Ann's place in the car and held onto her hat as Mr. Whittington drove off, still reminiscing. "I was born in Philadelphia, lived briefly in Indiana as a child, then returned to Philadelphia, where I lived for many years."

Liz said, "I enjoyed hearing about your time in England."

"I would not trade it for anything." His smile faded a bit. "Yet after my wife, Marilyn, passed away, I began to think about moving back to Indiana, as I recalled happy times here. Two months ago, I returned."

He appeared to savor Pleasant Creek's quaint downtown as they motored through, with its monolithic clock tower and brilliant flower beds, Swiss chalet-style buildings, and Amish buggies, their horses *clip-clopping* on the old brick streets. "I'd heard your town was perfectly lovely, but I had no idea."

"I haven't lived here very long, but I wouldn't want to move anywhere else." Liz couldn't resist probing. "Do you have relatives or friends in Pleasant Creek?"

"None that I know of. Despite my background in glass manufacture, I never have explored the state's rich history in glassmaking. When I retired, I promised myself that someday I would visit historical glass sites and museums to my heart's content. Perhaps find rare and unique glass for my collections."

Liz enjoyed their conversation as Reg purred along country roads through tasseled corn and yellowing soybean fields, past farm ponds encircled with necklaces of dainty Queen Anne's lace. She leaned back, the leather seat soft against her neck, the air cooling her face. But with more guests arriving the day after tomorrow, she should go back to the inn soon.

When she hinted at returning, her driver agreed. "I imagine Miss Sadie would like a ride in Reg as well."

Liz grinned. If they didn't return in thirty minutes on the dot, Sadie would scour the roads for them.

On the way back, Liz spotted her cousin Phoebe and her family in a buggy. As they entered downtown, she waved to her friends, Lydia and Dale King and their little girl, Addie, so cute in her white Amish *Kapp*.

She also spied a familiar tall figure walking near the clock tower. "Hi, Jackson!"

Jackson Cross, a furniture store owner and Pleasant Creek's mayor, stared as they drove past, his handsome face a snapshot of disbelief.

How do you like my hat, Jackson? It wasn't every day he—or anyone—saw her in old Hollywood mode, riding in a luxury vintage car with an elegant octogenarian scarecrow wearing a top hat.

A little mystique wouldn't hurt their . . . friendship? More-than-friendship?

She'd think about their relationship later. Liz turned to her fascinating guest, thanking him as they approached the inn's parking lot.

Sadie waited there, tapping her watch.

2

"We love this pumpkin quilt already, Mary Ann." Liz smoothed the orange, peach, cream, green, and brown prints she was basting together into a pumpkin shape. "You and Sadie really outdid yourselves this time."

"It will be gorgeous! Should bring in plenty of bids at the Harvest Festival auction." Twenty-something Caitlyn Ross, the youngest member of the Material Girls quilting group, ran her fingers over gold metallic fabrics and threads that would be worked into the whimsical pumpkin patch. They also would appear in a nighttime sky chock-full of stars and a round harvest moon.

"Plenty of bids sounds good. Plenty of money for Clothe Our Kids sounds even better." Mary Ann, always energized by a charitable cause, zipped around Sew Welcome's big, airy workroom.

"Where's Sadie?" Opal Ringenberg asked. "I could use her help cutting." This was nonsense; Opal, a purposeful woman in her seventies, cut fabric faster and better than anyone in the group.

"She's late." Mary Ann frowned. "I reminded her yesterday, before we rode with Mr. Whittington."

"She'll be here soon," Naomi Mason, about Liz's age, assured Mary Ann. "Sadie's all about making sure kids have coats for winter."

The Sew Welcome quilting maven nodded, but she glanced out the window again, her forehead folding into worry wrinkles.

Mary Ann had good reason to fret when Sadie didn't call or text. Her partner followed her own set of traffic rules, whether driving her Jeep, the gaudy Sew Welcome van, or riding her bright pink motorcycle.

Few other drivers argued with Sadie, including the local police, who preferred not to cross her.

Liz said, "She'll make it by refreshment time."

"Of course, she will." Naomi, seated at a sewing machine, shot Liz a meaningful look that said, *Let's change the subject.* "You went for a ride with a Mr. Whittington? Is he a guest?" Naomi asked.

Mary Ann answered before Liz could. "Yes, he's staying here, and he took us for rides in his beautiful old coupe."

"I thought I saw Liz in that fancy car driving past the clock tower." Opal's smile held rare mischief. "Saw the mayor too. You rattled him, I think."

"He did look surprised." Liz laughed.

Caitlyn, shaking her red-streaked hair, refused at first to taste Opal's triple-chocolate zucchini brownies. "Zucchini? My dad used to call it twentieth-century manna—during August, that's all we ate!"

"Have you tasted Opal's recipe?" Naomi took a big bite. "Mmmm."

Since Naomi was a baker, Caitlyn condescended to try one. Then two. Hugging Opal, Caitlyn admitted, "I was wrong. Please, please, please tell me to eat my vegetables."

Sadie finally appeared. "Sorry, everybody, but setting up my surprise took longer than I expected."

Surprise? Liz straightened. So did the other Material Girls.

Sadie's surprises could range from housing humanity's outcasts to stalking a wrongdoer with her trusty rifle, to making hats like her own wild, flowery concoctions for everyone—that she expected them to wear to church next Sunday.

Now she grabbed a brownie and gestured. "Come and see!"

Sadie darted out Sew Welcome's door. Liz exchanged glances with the other Material Girls. They followed Sadie through the four-season room to Liz's backyard.

Sadie threw her arms open wide. "Ta-da!"

A pop-up camper stood proudly in the waning light.

A pink camo pop-up camper.

"Isn't it *perfect*?" She hugged herself.

Well, as pink camo campers go . . . Liz nodded, smiling, as did the other Material Girls.

Though she privately wondered if Sadie planned to spend the night—or the week—in Liz's backyard.

"It certainly matches your Jeep." Mary Ann patted the canvas top.

"Oh, I know. And the inside is *so* cute. It's exactly what we need for our campout." She threw open the door and plunged inside.

Campout?

The group shared a questioning glance again—except for Opal. She set her mouth in a straight line.

Liz and Steve, her godson, had often hiked in state parks. He'd occasionally camped with friends. But Liz had never camped overnight, or even seen the interior of a camper.

So she followed Sadie inside for the grand tour. Mary Ann and Caitlyn crowded behind her, but there was only room for Mary Ann. It *was* cute, with two large beds covered in polka dot spreads on opposite ends, curtains, a table with bench seats, and a small refrigerator. There was very little floor space. Its low ceiling made Liz want to duck.

And everything was pink.

"There's a shower and a commode." Sadie flushed it to show that it worked.

Even the commode was pink.

Bunched in with the other women like celery stalks, Liz felt as if she'd been shut in a pink veggie drawer.

"The beds are sooo comfortable." Sadie dove onto the nearest one, posing with dazzling smile and hand on her hip as if part of a mattress ad.

Caitlyn and Naomi clamored to see the camper too, so Liz and Mary Ann exited.

"Did you see this coming?" Liz whispered to Mary Ann.

"Do I ever?"

Naomi, who didn't like close spaces any more than Liz, soon reappeared from the camper. Caitlyn and Sadie, chattering excitedly, made their way out.

"It sleeps six," Sadie said. "Two will have to sleep on the table, of course."

"On the table?" Liz wanted to be a good sport, but there were limits.

"Don't worry. It's covered with a nice mattress."

"This campout you're planning," Mary Ann said carefully. "When were you—?"

"For my birthday!" Sadie said. "You haven't forgotten, have you?"

"Of course not. It's August 12," Mary Ann said.

"That's when we'll camp. I told you that when I reserved our campsite last May at Pokagon State Park."

"You did no such thing." Mary Ann looked at her business partner skeptically.

"I did too." Sadie stuck out her chin. "I told all of you."

Silence.

Even Caitlyn stared. "Um, I don't think you told me."

"I *know* you didn't say anything to me." Mary Ann rechecked her phone's calendar, then held it out to Sadie. "See. I have your birthday down. Nothing about camping. And I always make *very* detailed notes."

"Oh, all right," Sadie muttered. "I forgot. But that's why I bought the camper. That's what I want to do on my birthday." She looked around the circle. "You'll all come, won't you?"

Liz wanted a signed statement that she wouldn't have to sleep on a table, but Sadie's hopeful face would have convinced her to sleep in a tent.

Maybe.

But who would take care of her B&B if she was gone overnight? Her mind quickly listed possible temporary innkeepers: her assistant, Sarah, and Sarah's husband, Isaac; Liz's cousin Miriam; or Aunt Ruth and one of her daughters.

Meanwhile, the other Material Girls checked their calendars.

Everyone promised to go, even Naomi, as long as she could get Jenny to come in at three thirty to help Candice Woodhouse bake.

All except Opal. "I'm sorry, Sadie. I have never enjoyed camping. I'm not about to start now."

"We're not backpacking in the Amazon," Sadie protested. "I'd just like us to all be together in my nice new camper. For my birthday."

"Sorry, Sadie," Opal repeated. "I'll go clean up the workroom."

Sadie exploded like a firecracker. "What, are you too snooty to go camping with us?"

"I'm not snooty," Opal retorted, though she'd raised her nose. "I just don't like camping. It's messy. It's muddy. I hate bugs."

"How about only overnight? One night instead of two?" Sadie pleaded.

"Sorry." Opal walked away.

Naomi and Caitlyn followed her, while Liz and Mary Ann hastened to soothe Sadie. But she shook off their attempts and yelled, "Well, what would you expect of someone who cheats to get a grand champion ribbon on her apron!"

Uh-oh. Liz wanted to cover her ears.

Opal, who never raised her voice, shouted, "I won fair and square!" She stomped into the inn.

Sadie stormed into her camper and yanked the curtains shut.

"Let her be for now." Mary Ann stopped Liz from following. "When those two dig up their apron grievances, it's no good talking to them."

Liz searched her memory. "What's with the aprons? I remember something about the county fair."

"The county fair back in the '60s, I heard." Mary Ann sighed. "Opal won the grand champion ribbon for the apron she sewed. Sadie has always insisted hers was better and that Opal won because her second cousin was the judge."

"Sadie and Opal are both so wonderful," Liz lamented. "I hate it when we Material Girls clash."

"They'll get over it." But Mary Ann's usual confident voice contained a note of doubt.

"We should go inside and help." Instead, Liz turned toward serene Jaynes Lake, reflecting the sun's colorful good night on its silvery surface. "Maybe we can unwind in the gazebo?"

"Good idea. Besides, Opal has probably cleaned the workroom from top to bottom already." Mary Ann chuckled weakly. "She works extra fast when she's mad."

Even as they approached the gazebo, the tightness in Liz's temples eased. She'd invested heavily in painting and repairing it, as well as surrounding it with lovely shrubs and flowers. The rose of Sharon bushes, covered with vivid pink, lavender, and white flowers, always looked spectacular in August. She and Mary Ann sat on the cushioned benches.

Ahhhh. Peace at last.

Then her eye caught movement nearby. A figure ducked behind a maple, then sneaked through a grove of trees. The inn's property stretched down to the lakeshore path. Most local people realized and respected that. As for tourists—her business depended on them. She didn't mind a few wanderers. This guy, however . . .

She pressed Mary Ann's arm, but her keen-eyed friend already had spotted the man. Together they watched his stealthy route toward the street.

A cold shiver spiraled down Liz's back. The man seemed to be checking out the inn.

"Stay here," Mary Ann hissed.

"What?"

Her friend might be in her sixties, but she could move. Before Liz could stir, Mary Ann had taken her own sneaky route. Halfway to the street, she hid behind a bush. She shook a finger at Liz, then slipped away again.

Obviously Mary Ann didn't want her presence. She wouldn't confront that guy alone, would she?

Liz checked to make sure her phone was in her pocket. Then she followed Mary Ann anyway, nearly catching her just as she met the man on the path.

"Oh, hello." Mary Ann flashed a toothy smile at the guy.

Liz ducked behind a huge burning bush. *Are you crazy?*

She pulled out her phone. Her finger hovered above speed dial to Chief Houghton of the Pleasant Creek police.

"Uh . . . hi." The guy sounded young. And uncomfortable. Liz peered around the bush. He was thin and dark-haired, pigeon-toed, and wearing hiking boots.

Mary Ann said, "I'm selling bingo tickets for charity. I'm *sure* you would like to buy some. Only twenty dollars for five. It's really for an excellent cause—to build a youth center to keep our young people out of trouble."

The man had made a few choking sounds as she continued her spiel, but he hadn't managed a word otherwise.

Apparently, he gave up, because Liz heard his footsteps *clump* the sidewalk in a fast walk, then almost a run.

Mary Ann called after him, "Are you sure you don't want to play bingo?"

Liz held back her laughter.

Mary Ann rounded the bush. "You were supposed to stay in the gazebo."

"What were you thinking, confronting a stranger? He could have been dangerous." Liz admonished.

"I had my keys in my pocket. I could have inflicted some damage with them." Mary Ann shrugged.

"That guy probably will avoid our street for a while."

"We'll probably have more trouble dealing with Sadie." Mary Ann sighed. "I wonder if she's still sulking in her camper."

"Let's see if she's cooled down."

She had—at least, enough that Liz and Mary Ann could coax her to spend the night at home in her air-conditioned farmhouse. The late-summer night's humidity swathed the town like a thick, damp quilt.

Watching the two partners head for the inn's parking lot together, Liz smiled.

But before she went to bed, she scanned the street and backyard. No Bingo Guy. She turned on the security lights outside.

And double-checked the inn's locks.

3

In her time as an innkeeper, Liz had provided lodging for every kind of guest she'd ever imagined, and then some: rabid basketball fans, old hippies, bikers, professional cyclists, her own ex-boyfriend from Boston—she scowled momentarily—and even a murderer or two.

The couple signing her register for a scheduled early arrival appeared top candidates for her Most Likely to Be Normal Award, surpassing even Tony Lanham. After Sadie and Opal's blowup, and Mary Ann's bingo ticket adventure the night before, normal was nice. She would put those two guest photos opposite Mr. Whittington's for sheer contrast.

Richard Fremont, a man in his fifties, wore pressed khakis and a subdued plaid shirt. His wife, Sandra, wore clear nail polish and carried a white cardigan, probably to ward off air-conditioning chills. The couple suffered no allergies, had no special diets, and the pleasant smiles that lit their faces appeared genuine. As Liz showed them to their room, they praised the inn and its antique furnishings.

"I'm so glad we have the Amish Room," Sandra enthused. "Look at this beautiful furniture and the hardwood floor. That quilt *has* to be handmade. And the lovely crock of yellow daisies—they light up the whole room."

"I'm glad you like it. We like to make our guests feel at home." Liz touched her flower arrangement with a finger, missing Kiera Williams, her gardener and flower-arranger extraordinaire, who had left to attend Indiana State University.

At least Sarah Borkholder, her young Amish assistant, would be in the area indefinitely, especially now that she was married. Even now, Sarah was doing her cleaning magic on the third floor.

Sandra set down her bag. "We're aching to explore downtown. I want to get an early start on my Christmas shopping."

Her husband gave an agreeable smile. He didn't seem to mind her shopping.

After Liz recommended Mama's Home Cooking for lunch, her guests departed.

Liz finished her morning tasks, wishing she could simply call her cousin Miriam and ask her to cover the inn during Sadie's campout. But Miriam and her husband, Philip, were members of the strict local Amish community and used their business phone for personal calls only in extreme emergencies.

Hoping she wouldn't interrupt Miriam's day too much, Liz drove to her farm.

Miriam and her daughters were up to their elbows in tomatoes, piled on every available space in Miriam's steamy kitchen, when Liz arrived. Huge kettles of water boiled on the woodstove, glowing with heat that seemingly doubled the temperature of the already hot day.

How did Amish women, in their long-sleeved, high-necked dresses, survive August? Liz still didn't know.

Yet Miriam, damp strands of brown hair curling around her red face, greeted Liz with a smile. "You are just in time to share a sandwich with us."

Despite Liz's protests, she found herself sitting in a rocker on the big white house's front porch, munching a thick sandwich of Miriam's homemade bread and a pickled vegetable relish made from her garden's tomatoes, onions, carrots, and cucumbers.

A visit with sweet young teenager Grace and Grace's lively younger sister, Keturah, always helped make Liz's day. The girls didn't seem to mind an interruption of their canning schedule.

Nor did Miriam. After sending the girls back into the kitchen to peel more tomatoes, Miriam spent a few quiet minutes rocking on the porch with Liz.

The relief on her cousin's tired face made Liz second-guess the request that had brought her here. What had she been thinking, asking Miriam to do more work? Liz shuffled Sadie's campout to the back of her mind.

However, Miriam, who had quickly become the sister she'd never had, zeroed in on Liz's reason for coming. "Can I help you in some way, cousin?"

Reluctantly, Liz told her. "I should have known you'd be canning this time of year. I can ask someone else." Though her other family candidates for the job were Amish too.

Miriam brushed off her concern. "The girls would love a night in your inn, as I would. We could not stay two nights—I doubt Philip and the boys could manage that long without us." Her smile held just a touch of mischief. "But I believe Philip will agree to one night."

"Thank you." Liz patted her arm. "It will mean so much to Sadie."

"I am always glad to help you." Miriam covered Liz's hand with her own. "You are family."

As she drove home past the Borkholder fields, Liz waved to Philip and his sons. Isaac, Sarah's husband, looked tanned, vigorous, and happy. Liz breathed a silent prayer of thanksgiving for the family she had only discovered upon moving to Indiana.

And that she could attend at least one night of Sadie's campout.

As Liz walked into the inn's rotunda, Mary Ann poked her head out of Sew Welcome. "Did you have a good time?"

"Wonderful." Liz took a second look at her friend. Where was the usual gleaming Mary Ann smile? "Is something wrong?"

"Afraid so." Now Mary Ann looked downright grim. "I talked to Chief Houghton. Last night, burglars trashed Lydia and Dale King's house."

"Burglars?" Liz's hand went to her mouth. Despite the difference in their ages—Lydia was in her twenties—she and Liz had become good friends while attending a Sew Welcome quilting class.

"They scrimped and saved for years to build and furnish that house, and those thugs tore it up from top to bottom in one night." Mary Ann's eyes flashed.

"Poor kids," Liz lamented. "They were gone, I hope."

Mary Ann nodded. "Both her parents were ill. Lydia and Dale had stayed the night to help out, and their daughter stayed with a friend."

"Did they let the chief look things over?" Liz asked.

Many of the area's Amish, unwilling to allow any armed intervention, avoided the police's help.

Mary Ann nodded. "Dale insisted, though both sets of parents objected."

A clash between her husband and their folks—just what Lydia needed on top of the upset of having her home invaded. "Sounds bad. Do you think they'll need more help cleaning up?"

"Of course their congregation will pitch in, but I've known Lydia since she was born, so I'm going to help as well." Mary Ann set her jaw. "I picked up work clothes at noon. Sadie will hold down the fort while I head out to their farm."

"I'll change and go with you." Liz couldn't imagine Lydia's feelings. How would she herself react if she'd come home to the destruction of her beautiful inn?

Liz donned the long denim skirt she often wore to Amish homes. She then set out covered plates of cookies in the sitting room, then hurried upstairs to ask Sarah to oversee coffee hour while she was at the Kings'.

That taken care of, Liz grabbed a loaf of banana bread from the freezer, then joined Mary Ann—who was armed with a picnic basket—and drove to the King farm.

When they pulled into the gravel driveway, Liz spotted three buggies parked near the barn. Help had already arrived. Liz smiled to see the reminder of the support that existed within the Amish community.

Stepping onto the farmhouse's wide front porch, Liz could hear voices speaking the customary Swiss Amish dialect through the screen door. A woman answered their knock, and several Amish men and women turned to eye them.

Mary Ann knew almost everyone at any Amish gathering and usually greeted them as old friends. Today, after scanning the rooms, Mary Ann stiffened. Liz pressed her lips together to keep from crying out.

The burglars had emptied closets and dumped out contents of the large china cabinet near the kitchen. Liz ached at the sight of broken crockery and glasses, probably wedding gifts. Worse, the intruders also had knocked large holes in the new house's walls and torn a number of boards from beautiful hardwood floors.

"Who would do something like this?" Mary Ann whispered.

Someone who was looking for something. Eyeing the floor's damage, Liz couldn't imagine anyone working that hard for the sake of mere destructiveness. No doubt Chief Houghton had figured that out. But did he have any idea what that something was?

"Liz. Mary Ann." Lydia stood at the bottom of the stairway. Small in stature and red-haired, with a sprinkling of freckles, she always looked younger than her twenty-six years. Today, her face dead white under a black Kapp, she resembled a lost waif.

Liz wanted to throw her arms around Lydia, but with a bevy of relatives present, she encircled her friend in the side hug acceptable to the Amish. "We're so sorry, Lydia."

Mary Ann enfolded her from the other side, and they silently shared the girl's pain.

Then Mary Ann said briskly, "What can we do to help?"

She and Liz got to work, aiding Lydia's mother-in-law, a sharp-eyed little woman, and Lydia's sisters-in-law in cleaning the kitchen. Food, pans, utensils, dishcloths, and towels had been thrown on the floor, all laced with molasses from crocks that had been upset. The pie safe had been turned upside down. The icebox was in the same state, with crocks of creamy milk turned over, adding to the molasses mess. The insides of plain but beautiful handmade cabinets had been hacked with an axe.

Only the big woodburning stove, its coals-only fire still heating the kitchen to nearly unbearable temperatures, looked intact. If it hadn't been made of iron, the vandals probably would have chopped it up too.

Thank heaven those creeps didn't start fires as part of their ugly game.

The hard work of scrubbing and cleaning kept her from bawling. The others probably felt the same way, though Liz read little in their impassive faces.

Little by little, the circle of devastation grew smaller. Scrubbing, laundering, and organizing, the women began to win battles against the sticky chaos. Men plastered walls and measured and stained boards for the floor and cabinets. The old-man lines in Dale King's young face began to fade.

Even Lydia regained a shadow of her usual self, mostly due to her daughter, Addie, a miniature pigtailed version of her mother, running in and out with a host of her little friends in their white Kapps.

With their sprightly presence, smiles crept back. *Thank the Lord for kids. They make us act like grown-ups, but keep us children at heart.*

Now Addie tugged on her mother's long, light-blue summer dress. "*Mutter*, can we play with my dolly's tea set?"

Dale's mother's eyebrows rose into her hairline.

Lydia, bent over a full dishpan, straightened. "I have no time to find toys, Addie. Go to the porch and play there."

The room's friendly buzz stilled at her atypical harshness. Addie's little pink mouth puckered. She skittered off, subdued friends hurrying in her wake.

A difficult day for this hurting family. Everyone focused studiously on their tasks.

But the expression Liz had read on Lydia's face spoke not only of fatigue, but something else—sheer panic. That was an odd reaction to the child's request. Was Addie somehow out of line?

The grandmother had looked uptight too. Maybe Lydia's mother-in-law made life more difficult for Lydia than Liz realized.

Don't be nosy, Liz chastised herself. And she was probably imagining things. Lydia was just reacting to a super-tough day. She didn't need an amateur's psychoanalysis.

At suppertime, the women loaded outdoor makeshift tables with a delicious meal, with plenty of leftovers for the King family. Operating with their usual efficiency, they and the children cleared up and washed dishes while the men dismantled the tables, carried chairs back into the house, and helped Dale do chores.

At twilight, when kerosene lamps were lit and children chased fireflies across the yard, the Kings expressed their thanks in typical understated language. Some of their helpers hitched up horses and collected belongings and children. Liz noticed Dale's brothers remained while their families went home.

What did Amish guard duty look like? No one here carried weapons.

But Chief Houghton and his officers no doubt would also patrol the area with sharp eyes looking out for trouble.

"I hope they have a quiet night," Mary Ann said as she pulled out onto the road.

Liz nodded. "At least they have beds they can sleep in and food for a day or two."

When she arrived home, Liz made sure all her doors and windows were locked, and all the outside lights were on.

She felt safe here.

If only Lydia and her family could feel safe too.

4

Entering the rotunda after breakfast the next day, Liz saw Tony Lanham kneeling beside Beans again, the bulldog grunting with pleasure as Tony rubbed his belly.

As she moved to the rotunda's desk, Liz spotted Sadie peeking out the window in Sew Welcome's door. How long before Sadie barreled out insisting the bulldog needed his daily twenty hours of sleep?

Liz glanced at her watch. A visit to Sweet Everything ordinarily would present an escape from such stress. But today, Mary Ann had summoned Liz to the bakery to try to talk Opal around in regard to Sadie's birthday.

The bell over Sweet Everything's entrance jingled as Liz entered. Her friend, pouring coffee for a customer, caught Liz's glance at the cupcakes in her glass case.

"Key lime, right?" Naomi gestured with her head. "You'll need it. They're in the back corner."

Given the way Naomi raised her sculpted eyebrows as she spoke, Liz considered ordering two.

She paused, absorbing the charm of the soft-gray walls, white tables and chairs, coral-colored paper place mats, and the fresh coral-tinted carnations that were Naomi's signature decor style.

Then Liz steeled herself and marched to the back of the dining area, where Mary Ann and Opal sat. Mary Ann was indulging in a chocolate éclair. Opal was drinking black coffee, looking righteous and immovable as the local Amish bishop.

Liz greeted them and told about her visit with Miriam—minus

her cousin's campout-covering agreement. Naomi brought Liz's coffee and cupcake, and they all chatted.

After a few minutes of pleasantries, Opal crossed her arms. "I know what you're trying to do, and it won't work. I am *not* camping."

"Oops. Someone's at the counter." Naomi deserted them.

Mary Ann stirred her coffee. "Well, of course, that's up to you, Opal. But you're a Material Girl. One of us." She leveled her best all-for-one look at her recalcitrant friend. "I'm not sure what we'll do without you."

"You'll get sweaty and mosquito-bitten and rained on just the same," Opal said. "And *dirty*."

"But Sadie's camper has a shower," Mary Ann said.

"It's the size of a shoe box," Opal retorted, "and if you want to spend half a day standing in line, waiting for a shower—*and* a toilet—enjoy it."

Yikes. She's madder than I thought. Liz crammed a big bite into her mouth.

"I stood in line way too much as a kid. I was the oldest of ten, remember?" Opal glared. "And my dad's idea of fun was camping too. Never again."

"But you can be first in line," Mary Ann promised, "after the birthday girl, of course."

Opal stuck out her dimpled chin.

Mary Ann's never-say-die smile faded a little. She cast a glance at Liz, as if to say, "You try."

What can I do? Liz swallowed and attempted a different approach. "You and Sadie have been friends all your lives, Opal. This would mean the world to her."

Opal sputtered, "That's exactly why she shouldn't have pushed this on me. Sadie knows perfectly well how I feel about camping. Yet she set all this up, expecting me to cave. Well, she can forget it."

"Think about singing around the campfire with your friends," Liz urged, "and eating s'mores—"

"I'll never get the smoky smell out of my clothes. Gooey marshmallows and chocolate get in my hair," Opal's voice rose to rare loudness, "and Sadie couldn't sing on key if her life depended on it." She stood. "Once and for all, I. Am. Not. Going. Camping. Ever."

She sailed out of Sweet Everything with her nose in the air, leaving a wake of curious stares that found their way back to Mary Ann and Liz.

Naomi wandered over with the coffeepot. "Need a refill?"

"*Now* you show up." Liz eyeballed her friend. "Where were you in our hour of need?"

Naomi returned the look. "Could I have changed Opal's mind?"

"I doubt it." Even ever-optimistic Mary Ann wilted.

"I'll take seconds on the cupcake. And more coffee," Liz said.

———— *⁓⁓⁓⁓⁓⁓⁓⁓⁓⁓* ————

Please let this coffee hour go well, Liz thought later. She was still sugared up from her visit to the bakery, and it was making her anxious.

At their first sight of Mr. Whittington, wearing a red soccer jersey along with his top hat and plaid slippers, Richard and Sandra halted at the sitting room door. But Whittington's charming smile drew them in, and soon they were chatting like old friends.

Sadie, who arrived a few minutes later, was at her funny best. She and Mr. Whittington played off each other like professional comics.

"Stop! I can't laugh anymore," Richard gasped, holding his sides.

His wife had giggled until she couldn't speak.

Liz's sides ached from laughing too, but after the earlier fiasco with Opal, she'd take the pain.

After the Fremonts left for an evening with relatives, Mr. Whittington, with a courtly tip of his hat, addressed Sadie. "Dear lady, I have enjoyed this time immensely. Would you care to share dinner with me and extend our evening of story and mirth?"

"I had fun too. Sounds like a plan." Sadie donned her latest find, a huge straw hat with giant sunflowers and purple pansies. The two decided to take advantage of the all-you-can-eat spaghetti special at Mama's Home Cooking.

Liz watched the free spirits walk downtown, a few drivers slowing their cars to scrutinize as they passed.

Thank you, Mr. Whittington and Sadie, for a great ending to a tough afternoon.

Liz cleared up and pondered how she could procrastinate longer on finishing the inn's budget spreadsheets. She wasn't hungry at the moment, but later she'd eat a piece of fruit and maybe a sandwich for supper. But only one overripe banana remained in the dining room's fruit bowl. She'd walk to the farmer's market on the other side of downtown and replenish her supply. Maybe she could stop at Harvey's Antiques and see what was new.

Early evening heat waves rippled over downtown, and she quickly moved to the shady side of the street. But the ripe pears, peaches, and blackberries she bought made the trip worth it.

So did the lovely dishes she'd spotted at the antiques store. For months she'd been seeking a set that would enhance her dining room's deep colonial blue. This seventy-five-year-old, blue floral pattern looked like a perfect match. Harvey wanted her to purchase his three extra place settings as well, but the set of twelve would more than fill her table, even when extended. She bought what she wanted at a good price.

"I'll pick them up before you close," she promised. Clearly happy to make a sale, Harvey agreed.

Afterward, Liz passed Mama's Home Cooking. Sadie and Mr.

Whittington sat at a table next to the front windows, laughing so hard they didn't notice her wave.

As she continued through downtown, though, unease prodded her. Liz found herself listening, watching, as if she were in an unfamiliar city instead of Pleasant Creek's square.

Chill, Liz. What's the matter with you?

Liz scanned the sidewalks and shops, well peopled during early evening, as tourist season was still at its peak. Clusters of shoppers carried totes heavy with treasures. Young parents with strollers chatted and watched their children play around the clock tower's grounds.

Why did she feel this odd tension?

A smartly dressed businessman, probably on his way home from the office, waited at the light on the other side of the street, along with a man and woman herding a Little League team, a task she did not envy. She waved to her pastor and his family, as well as her uncle Amos, driving past with his big horses and wagon. *See, Liz? It's just a normal evening.*

She nearly jumped out of her skin when a male voice behind her called her name.

"Sorry." Jackson Cross took a step back. "I didn't mean to scare you."

She laughed. "I'm jumpy for some silly reason."

"Maybe you need a little treat to settle you down." He gestured toward a stand near the clock tower that sold the world's best homemade ice cream.

"That's exactly what I *don't* need." Liz chuckled ruefully. When she told him about her double-cupcake morning, he caved.

"Then maybe a walk by the lake?" His hazel eyes sparkled as he said it, and his smile accentuated his square jaw.

With this weird nervousness, she'd welcome his presence, but she couldn't ignore her responsibilities. "I'm afraid I have lots to do this evening. And I need to stop and pick up a purchase at Harvey's. Maybe you could give me a lift?"

She really liked Jackson, but she wasn't sure where they stood. Nor where she wanted them to stand. She had so much going on with the inn that she probably didn't need to add a relationship to the mix right now.

"Okay." His lower lip stuck out the least bit, adding a little boy's appeal to his good looks, and Liz nearly changed her mind. But the walk back to Jackson's furniture store to retrieve his old truck turned out to be just right.

Later, as they drove back to the inn with the china safely in the back, she told him about her upcoming first-time campout with the Material Girls, and Jackson soon had her laughing as he related the worst of his Boy Scout adventures. At the inn, he insisted on carrying her new china inside and helping her wash it and put it away.

They lingered at her door a few minutes before saying good night.

From a covert spot inside near the sitting room windows, she watched Jackson walk back to his truck. His strong presence had dispersed her silly fears.

Or *were* they silly? Something during her trip downtown continued to niggle at her, but refused to identify itself.

It'll come back to me. Vague impressions like these usually solidified sooner or later.

But did she want them to?

Liz wasn't sure.

———— ————

Liz woke feeling as if she'd slept in a sauna.

Sweaty from head to toe, Liz threw aside the damp sheet and groped till she found her clock. Five thirty. She turned off the six thirty alarm.

When she dragged herself to the thermostat, it read eighty-three degrees—though set ten degrees below that. She groaned.

Air-conditioning problems in August? They couldn't happen at a worse time.

No amount of fiddling awakened her dormant central air. Liz threw open windows, threw on clothes, and hurried from her apartment into the rotunda and common areas. She opened more windows, letting in morning air she hoped would cool the place until she could summon a repairman.

Liz revised her breakfast menu—no sizzling bacon or biscuits today. Instead, she'd set out cold ham, cheeses, and chilled fruit.

She called Naomi, knowing her friend had risen two hours earlier to bake, and told her about the problem. "I need your best stuff to get my guests through the morning. Whatcha got?"

"Chocolate croissants. Cinnamon pear muffins with walnuts turned out well too."

The day looked better already. "I'll take a half dozen of the muffins and a dozen croissants."

"Chocolate gets us through anything." Naomi chuckled.

The pastries, along with the relatively cool morning breeze, did seem to help her guests take the inconvenience in stride.

Sandra munched a second croissant. "Delicious! These are the best I've ever eaten."

Her husband agreed as he worked on his third.

"Looks like a good day for the Auburn car museum and indoor flea market," Richard said cheerfully. "I can't wait to check out all those vintage cars."

"Wonderful exhibits," Mr. Whittington agreed. "Auburn is where they made my '31 coupe, you know."

"That cool old car out in the parking lot?" In the subsequent enthusiastic conversation, Richard, Mr. Whittington, and Tony Lanham seemed to forget about the heat.

If only Liz's efforts to find a repairman went as well as breakfast. Neither Calvin nor Stefan—handymen she'd called on occasionally in the past—was available. Every phone call to a heating and air-conditioning company generated a similar response: "Sorry, ma'am, can't get you in for a couple of days."

After a while, she wondered if she was reaching the same recording.

Liz called friends to borrow fans, but if this situation continued, she'd have to buy a bunch from the hardware store. Her budget spreadsheets wouldn't like that.

With all the hassle, she'd almost forgotten Tony was leaving this morning. She entered the rotunda to find him performing what had become Beans's favorite morning ritual: a major belly rub and ear scratch.

Liz smiled as she watched them from the desk. Tony, his duffel tossed carelessly by his side, acted like a ten-year-old leaving for summer camp. She said, "Beans certainly will miss you."

"Uh—about that." Tony stood and cleared his throat. "I know you love him—shoot, everybody does! But I wondered if . . . Would you consider selling him to me?"

Liz blinked, then blinked again. Her favorite rug without Beans collapsed on it? No daily doggy duty at the crack of dawn? The thoughts both excited and pained her.

Sadie appeared, her face turning red. "Beans is *not* for sale!"

Of course she'd been watching Tony's every move. And her eavesdropping abilities had only increased with the years.

"Now, Sadie—" Liz tried to soothe her friend.

"Don't you 'now, Sadie' me, Liz." Sadie seemed to have grown six feet, towering over the stunned businessman. "This is Beans's *home*. How can you offer to *buy* him?"

Tony looked from Liz to Sadie to Liz again, forehead crinkled. He finally spoke. "I'm sorry. I didn't realize—" He picked up his duffel. "Bye, fella. Thanks, Liz."

He almost bolted out the front door.

"The nerve of that guy." Sadie almost collapsed on top of the bulldog. She cooed, "*Buy* you? How could he even think of such a thing? Crazy. Bonkers." Hugging Beans like a stuffed animal, she shot an accusing glance at Liz. "Where do you *get* these people?"

Liz closed her eyes. "I have no idea."

Her phone rang. Trying to clear her head, she answered.

"Ms. Eckardt? This is Dave from Samson's Cooling and Heating. I got your message."

Could the day actually take an upturn? "Yes, the air-conditioning has gone out in my bed-and-breakfast. My guests are sweltering. Can you come and fix it?"

"Sure."

Her heart leaped.

"In a couple of days . . ."

Same recording. Liz drooped.

Sadie crooned.

Exhausted from all the love, Beans snored.

———

Smoothies.

In a few hours, Liz would make smoothies for coffee hour instead of baking cookies and heating the kitchen—and herself—another three hundred fifty degrees. Liz turned her wet face toward the fan she'd mounted on her rotunda desk, wishing the air it blew didn't feel like it had come from a rain forest.

Still, fans could be fun when no one was around. Liz glanced around the rotunda, then stuck her nose close to the fan.

"Aaaah-h-h-h." Her voice droned through its blurred blades as it hadn't since she was eight.

An innkeeper had to find her fun any way she could, right?

Liz was searching the Internet for smoothie recipes when Mary Ann emerged from Sew Welcome. Did the woman ever sweat? Liz had given up on makeup, but Mary Ann's looked committee-meeting perfect, as always.

"No luck on the air-conditioning?" Mary Ann's voice held a note of sympathy.

Liz shook her head. "Sorry the heat is scaring your customers away. I'm hoping a repairman will come tomorrow." She lowered her voice. "This is way, way too much like camping, right?"

Mary Ann clicked her tongue. "I'm afraid so. Let's just pray the weather breaks before we go."

"I don't know how the Amish do it every summer." Liz fanned herself with a file folder. "Miriam and her girls are probably canning a few hundred quarts of stuff today."

"They don't consider the heat a problem," Mary Ann agreed. "Canning, cooking, ironing." Her smooth forehead puckered. "Right now, though, the Wickeys are dealing with something far worse. Someone broke into their house yesterday."

Liz stared. "Another burglary? When?"

"It happened while they were gone to a barn raising overnight."

Such a shame. Liz didn't know the Wickeys, but she imagined they were a typical, hardworking Amish family. "Was anything stolen?"

"I've heard several versions of what happened. Some include a missing horse, cows, and salable items from the barn and house." Mary Ann's mouth thinned to a straight line. "But whoever did it seemed bent on trashing the place."

"Who would do such a thing?" Already steaming, Liz's temperature rose.

"Who knows?" Mary Ann shook her head. "Of course, everyone's pointing a finger at outsiders."

"I'll bet it was." Sadie poked her head out of Sew Welcome. "I read in the Fort Wayne paper last week that robberies in Wildton and the towns near it were traced to Detroit."

Though we have our share of homegrown trouble. The last thing Liz had anticipated in moving to Pleasant Creek had been helping the police solve local mysteries. She said, "The Kings cooperated with Chief Houghton. Do you think the Wickeys will?"

"If a horse was stolen, they might be more likely to let Houghton in on it. I hope they do." Mary Ann seemed to understand her Amish friends' convictions. But that didn't keep her from worrying about them.

She and Sadie returned to Sew Welcome, and Liz tried to focus on smoothies once more. But she couldn't help thinking of the Amish farms surrounding Pleasant Creek that helped make it a lovely, peaceful community.

A community that boasted plenty of good guys too. They would track down these burglars so it could stay that way.

With visions of her cousin Miriam and her sweet family, not to mention motherly Aunt Ruth, Liz certainly hoped so.

5

If only everyone in the world were like Sandra and Richard Fremont. The next morning, as they prepared to leave, they didn't mention a word about their less-than-perfect stay.

"Thanks for your flexibility." Liz presented them with a reduced bill. "I wish I could have found a repairman so you could have enjoyed more than one comfortable day here."

Richard's "it-was-nothing" gesture downplayed the air-conditioning disaster. "We spent most of the time sightseeing elsewhere."

"Our time here reminded us of when we were kids." Sandra's ever-present smile reassured Liz. "Big house, small town, windows open, frogs croaking, that incredible summer-night fragrance—"

"Besides, I had fun playing with the fans." Grinning, Richard leaned into Liz's desk fan. "Aaah-h-h-h-h."

What an upbeat couple. Liz laughed with them and waved as they departed.

Fortunately, Mr. Whittington, her only remaining guest, seemed to take the heat in stride as well. He'd resorted to wearing plaid Bermuda shorts along with his top hat.

"Old knobby knees are not a pretty sight." The elderly man slapped them as he descended the stairs. "But it is a bit sultry in here, you know."

Yes, she knew.

"Besides, I'm off to a tour of the glass factory in Kokomo," he continued. "I imagine it will be rather warm, with furnaces heating the glass and all."

Enjoy. Apparently, his interest in glass trumped even this hot day.

As she watched Mr. Whittington drive off in his coupe, she recalled his other day trips to area museums. She and Sarah, in cleaning his room, had noticed groupings of glass vases and knickknacks, some of which appeared antique—a collection that seemed to grow daily.

He'd also brought a record player with him and a collection of 1950s albums he often played.

Mr. Whittington ranked near the top of her Quirky Guest List. But the name of her next arrivals—they would come Sunday evening—piqued Liz's curiosity: Brumpett, Maxine and Marlene. Were they sisters? They were probably older ladies, given their first names.

Would they wear Scottish plaid Bermuda shorts too?

She shuddered. Surely, by Sunday, her air-conditioning woes would end.

However, her own troubles couldn't compare to those of the Kings or the Wickeys. As Liz recalled the burglaries, the murky mood that had shadowed her farmer's market trip earlier that week returned.

Cleaning the Rose of Sharon Room in preparation for the Brumpetts, Liz found herself reviewing every detail of her walk through downtown while she'd been carrying her bag of fruit. She'd seen women shopping, a businessman with an interesting gait crossing the street, young parents with strollers, and friends and relatives. Finally, she'd run into Jackson, who temporarily eased her absurd nervousness.

Ten minutes later, even as Liz rejoiced in a phone call from a repairman who could come tomorrow, the unease persisted.

Back in her quarters, she turned on an old sitcom rerun to combat it. And then she remembered.

She'd experienced similar anxiety even earlier that week—when Mary Ann accosted that man sneaking around her property near the lake.

But she hadn't seen him downtown.

Or had she?

Liz caught her breath.

Pigeon toes.

The guy who had glared at Mary Ann's bingo-ticket push had stood with hiking boot toes definitely turned in.

The businessman at the stoplight . . . his stance had matched Bingo Guy's. Perfectly.

You're jumping to conclusions. Lots of people were pigeon-toed. Besides, the two men didn't resemble each other in any other way.

The carefully dressed businessman had looked older and heavier, with sandy hair and beard. He was also taller than Bingo Guy, who surely measured under six feet.

But all these were superficial differences that could be created with skillful wig and clothing changes. Even the height disparity could be generated by higher heels.

She certainly had seen no proof of such a masquerade. But if she was right, why would someone go to such trouble to disguise himself?

She needed to talk this out, slow the mental merry-go-round spinning out of control in her head. But whom should she call?

Both Opal and Caitlyn, though decades apart in age, would shake their heads at the improbability of Liz's idea. Mary Ann already had shrugged off Bingo Guy as unimportant, and certainly not dangerous. Sadie? Liz closed her eyes. Sadie would hunt for him in her Jeep, brandishing her shotgun.

But Naomi would listen and ponder with her. And not have her committed.

Knowing her friend retired early, Liz hurriedly pulled out her phone.

"Sure, I won't go to bed for another couple of hours." Naomi's warm, laid-back voice already soothed Liz. "Want me to bring something? I have peach custard tarts left—"

"No! I've been eating way too much sugar lately."

"Gotcha. No peach tarts." Naomi's tone lost some of its levity. "Sounds important."

"Maybe. Maybe it's nothing. But let's meet at the gazebo. I need fresh air and a good sunset."

Only after she'd hung up did Liz remember that she and Mary Ann had been sitting in the gazebo when they first noticed Bingo Guy. She shivered. Then laughed.

Thanks to Mary Ann, she doubted he would return.

Leaving the stuffy apartment for the breezy openness of her backyard lifted Liz's spirits. The spectacular sunset reminded her that God had managed the universe for some time. He would continue to do so, regardless of whether two men's pigeon-toed stances spelled trouble or not.

Naomi soon arrived, and they sat in the gazebo, breathing in the lakeside landscape.

"I needed this," Naomi murmured, leaning back on the bench. "Sometimes it seems that summer leaves before I get a chance to play outside."

Liz let her hardworking friend enjoy the evening awhile.

Then Naomi turned her sympathetic, brown-eyed gaze on Liz. "Okay. Spill."

Her friend hadn't heard about Mary Ann's encounter with Bingo Guy, and, as Liz expected, Naomi alternately gasped and giggled. "That woman has *moxie*! A normal person would have called the cops and then run."

She sobered quickly though as Liz described her uncharacteristically anxious trip through downtown and the businessman and his pigeon-toed stance, so similar to Bingo Guy's.

For a minute, Naomi said nothing, and Liz feared her fellow Material Girl would think the heat had affected her brain.

Instead, Naomi ventured, "I think I've seen him too."

"You're kidding." Liz sat up straight. "Where?"

"At the bakery. Yesterday afternoon."

"You noticed the stance?" Either she and Naomi were unusually observant or exceptionally nosy.

"Yeah," Naomi frowned. "I'd just poured more coffee for Mr. Whittington—he's such a funny old man—"

"He is," Liz agreed. In a few short days, her guest had befriended half of Pleasant Creek.

"Then several customers came in at once, and I had to hustle." She frowned. "I don't recall that particular man's face. His hair might have been dark, with some gray. I think he wore glasses. He kind of faded into the background. Didn't eat anything, only drank house coffee, black. But I noticed the way he stood, though his condition wasn't nearly as bad as my friend's daughter's. She had to have surgery."

That explained Naomi's powers of perception. *Maybe* I'm *the only nosy one.*

But Liz's gut insisted they'd noticed something significant. She chewed her lip. "So—if these three men are all the same person, why the disguises?"

"Maybe he's casing downtown for future break-ins?" Naomi gulped. "If he is, your inn and my bakery are on his list."

"But the only recent burglaries I've heard about have been at Amish farms." Liz tried to laugh. "Perhaps he doesn't want to leave anyone out—an equal opportunity burglar."

Naomi gave her a strange look. "I suppose . . ."

Liz shook her head. "Maybe the heat *has* gotten to me. These three might very well be different men who happen to share a slight posture problem. As for burglaries—only one guy acted suspiciously. The others probably have nothing whatsoever to do with the Amish break-ins."

Naomi eyeballed her. "Then why does this bother you so much?"

"I don't know." Liz exhaled. "The air-conditioning guy's coming tomorrow. Maybe after one full night of cool, refreshing sleep, I'll stop stalking pigeon-toed people and seeing burglars peeking from every corner."

"So you're not going to tell Chief Houghton about all this?"

"Houghton? I could barely bring myself to tell you." Liz shrugged. "Mary Ann didn't seem to regard Bingo Guy as a threat."

Naomi laughed ruefully. "She's one awesome lady, but not everybody in the world can be managed with pie or discount bingo tickets." Naomi's hands folded under her chin. "We could go together to see the chief, if you want."

"You'd go with me?" Liz said. "He already thinks I'm half loony. And that I attract trouble like a picnic draws ants. Why incriminate yourself as well?"

"He doesn't think you're loony," Naomi said. "You've helped him with a bunch of cases, and he trusts your instincts."

Liz shook her head. "I've stumbled into situations more than I've figured them out."

"Well, you may have stumbled onto something important here." Naomi refused to back off. "Look at it this way: When burglaries happen in small towns, policemen want to know about suspicious strangers."

Bingo Guy *had* slunk around her property before Mary Ann dispatched him. Liz drummed her fingers on the bench. "I suppose I could tell him about that incident."

"Absolutely." Naomi smiled encouragingly.

"Then I'd better do it now, before I talk myself out of it."

They stood and walked to the police station.

Tonight Chief Houghton manned the front counter, a spot usually staffed by one of his officers.

"No help tonight?" Liz had hoped she could mention Bingo Guy to one of the lesser guys and leave.

The chief's smile seemed tired. "Gerst's on vacation, and Dixon's wife just had a baby. So Hughes and I are holding the fort."

"I heard you have a new granddaughter too." Naomi knew as much about Pleasant Creek's news as Mary Ann did. "Congratulations!"

"Thanks." His eyes twinkled, though Liz, echoing Naomi's sentiments, noticed they were bloodshot. "But I don't get any more sleep than Dixon. Wife has this idea she needs to help with the baby around the clock. At our house." Now his lined jowls sagged. "Kenzie's cute as a button, but she's got colic. Hasn't stopped screaming since she was born." He rubbed a hand over his face, then appeared to shake off his sleeping troubles. "What can I do for you ladies?"

Definitely not a day to present wild theories, but it had to be done. Liz said, "I heard about the break-ins on the Amish farms. While this probably has nothing to do with it, I thought I'd tell you."

He waved a weary hand. "Sure. Shoot."

Quickly, she related the Bingo Guy incident.

He sat on a stool and linked his hands on the counter. "And?"

"Uh—that's all." *Quick, Naomi, let's beat it.*

"No, it isn't." He exhaled. "You never come here with one simple little incident. If I know you, there is definitely more."

She fidgeted. "I'm not sure about this at all—"

"Let's hear it. But first, I made coffee. You ladies want a cup?"

They declined politely, though Liz knew Naomi, barista extraordinaire, stifled a gag as Houghton poured coffee that looked like motor oil into a stained mug.

The chief downed half the mug's contents in one gulp. "Okay. Now tell me."

Liz did. Naomi added her contribution.

Chief Houghton's fingers drummed on the counter. "I see."

Translation: Have you finally gone over the edge? "I know it sounds disjointed and a little crazy, but—"

"More than a little." He grimaced. "But I'll keep it in mind. You're not often wrong."

Liz and Naomi left.

Walking back to Sweet Everything, they didn't say much.

Why did I let you talk me into this? Liz wouldn't express her annoyance out loud, but she wished she hadn't listened to her friend.

Or did she?

"Feel better?" Naomi clasped her hands as if in appeal, but a grin tugged at her mouth.

"Yes." Despite Houghton's less-than-enthusiastic reaction, Liz felt as if she'd dropped a heavy pack. "Yes, I do. No more playing ping-pong with what-ifs until I can't think straight. Houghton knows about it, and I can forget about it."

"Right." Naomi squeezed her arm. "Now relax. Take a swim. Watch TV."

"Sounds like a plan." A dip in the lake would cool her down.

After her refreshing swim, Liz's cell rang. To her amazement, a repairman offered to evaluate the problem that evening instead of tomorrow.

Even more amazing, the repair proved to be minor—and inexpensive. By bedtime, Liz's air-conditioning unit was rumbling cheerfully, the inn comfortable as a spring morning.

"That feels lovely." Mr. Whittington, returning from his day trip, breathed in the coolness. "I am happy for you, dear lady, for me, and for the rest of the world. No more shorts!"

Things really did fall into place sometimes. To celebrate, Liz planned a menu of sausage, biscuits, and gravy the next morning. After setting out dry ingredients and pans, she would go into her quarters and, with any luck, enjoy the best sleep she'd experienced in days.

The kitchen's landline rang. Liz, pulling her black spider skillet from a cabinet, frowned as she *clumped* it onto the counter. The Material Girls usually called her cell, especially after nine. She didn't recognize this number. Maybe someone with a last-minute plea for a room?

"Olde Mansion Inn, Liz speaking."

Silence.

"Hello?"

Breathing, deep and hoarse.

Liz slammed the phone. *So adolescent.*

She shook off annoyance and went to her quarters, where she dove into her comfy bed, anticipating sweet, wonderful sleep.

But slumber did not come until after two more strange phone calls—from different numbers. Long after unplugging the landline, she lay awake.

If only she could unplug her mind.

6

"Not a restful night, my dear?" Mr. Whittington, accepting breakfast from Liz, cocked his head. His usually twinkly eyes softened. "Such a shame."

"Oh, a couple of late phone calls woke me up." Liz brushed aside his—and her own—concern. "I'll grab a nap this afternoon."

"Thank you for this lovely breakfast. But you put entirely too much effort into it. May this Sabbath bring you rest and refreshment."

His kindness helped clear her foggy head. Why had she let those stupid phone calls get to her? Everyone experienced those from time to time.

When the old gentleman asked if he could accompany her to church, she enjoyed their fun ride in his coupe, the morning breeze wafting through her hair.

At Pleasant Creek Community Church, Mr. Whittington attracted more than a few discreet stares, with his long-tailed coat, big red bow tie, plaid slippers, and top hat. One child even asked him if he was the Cat in the Hat. He readily charmed them all.

Her guest appeared to listen intently to Pastor Brad's sermon, and he sang a mellow bass to hymns and contemporary choruses alike. Sensing Mr. Whittington's enjoyment, Liz relaxed, letting the Scriptures comfort, yet challenge her. *Refreshing? Restful? Definitely.*

After church, she savored the sleep she craved—a nap that lasted just long enough. Then Liz went upstairs to make sure the Rose of Sharon Room was ready for the Brumpetts.

The door of the Somewhere in Time Room opened. Mr. Whittington beckoned. "May I show you something, Liz?"

His secretive smile roused her curiosity. "Certainly. My new arrivals won't be here for a few hours."

She entered and took the chair Mr. Whittington indicated. He pulled a large, elegant black brocade box from under his bed, removing its satin elastic band and cover as he sat in a rocker beside her.

She gasped. Nestled in the box's velvety lining was a gilt-edged tea set. The teapot, creamer and sugar bowl, cookie plate, and eight cups and saucers all were a size above the usual child's set, yet not big enough for adults. Were they custom-made?

Mr. Whittington picked up the lavender-and-white teapot and showed her its craftsmanship.

A delicate butterfly, its wings finely detailed with lavender, purple, and pale yellow, appeared to have landed on the top, serving as the lid's handle. Smaller butterflies had landed on the sugar bowl and creamer tops, and they fluttered across the saucers and cookie plate as well.

Liz gently ran her fingers over the fine china. "What an incredibly beautiful set. Where did you find it?"

"I did not have to search." His smile did not reach his sad eyes. "My father, James Whittington, designed it years ago as a birthday gift for my only child, Sherry. See his initials on the bottom of the cup? He put them on every piece he created."

The tiny letters were wrought with the same precision and delicacy as the cup. "What an artist!"

"He was indeed. I possess his passion for glass and china, but regrettably, I did not inherit his talent."

"Your daughter must have been amazingly careful for it to have survived intact."

"She was. Very early, she seemed to understand its value. Sherry loved the set and used it only for special occasions—even her high school graduation party." Again, that sorrowful smile. "Unfortunately, she died years ago. She was only in her twenties."

"I am so sorry, Mr. Whittington." How sad, to have lost both his wife and his only child.

"Thank you." He leaned forward, his eyes wistful. "Do you have time to listen to a little more of the set's history?"

"Certainly." Perhaps he would explain why he'd brought the tea set to Pleasant Creek.

Mr. Whittington settled back into his chair, gazing beyond Liz as if looking into the past. "Actually, my father made two sets, the first one decades before the one he made for Sherry. When he was a young man, learning the glass and china business with his father in Philadelphia, he fell in love with an Amish girl named Sally Kauffman, whom he met on holiday near Lancaster. Of course, both families were intensely opposed to a marriage. In spite of that—or perhaps because of it—they had a child out of wedlock, a little girl they named Priscilla. Sally was shunned for a time, forced to live with an unbaptized relative. Father visited her and their baby often, despite his family's opposition. When Priscilla was quite small, he designed the first tea set for her, in shades of rose and lavender.

"Father hoped against hope he and Sally could yet marry, even when my grandfather sent him to England, ostensibly for business reasons. But while Father was overseas, Sally renounced their relationship. My guess is that it was just too hard for her to raise the child alone, and she missed her family's support. She was reinstated by her Amish community when a more forgiving bishop assumed leadership. Sally married an Amish man, Solomon Hertzler, who adopted Priscilla. When Father returned, they had moved, and her family refused to tell him where. He tried for years to find Priscilla, but never did."

"How very awful for him." Liz, who had come from Boston to

seek her mother's family among the Amish, had succeeded. How sad for James, who had not.

"Ten years later, Father fell in love with and married my mother, Kathryn, and I was born. So he still experienced plenty of love and happiness." Mr. Whittington's mischievous smile returned. "When Sherry was born, Father could not wait to begin work on a tea set for her. He gave her this set for her first birthday, before she could even drink out of a cup!"

A typical grandpa. Liz chuckled at Mr. Whittington's account of Sherry's preschool tea parties with her grandfather James.

Liz had carried a family quilt and her mother's diary from Boston in her search for family, a quest that led her to her relatives. Would this tea set bring Mr. Whittington a happy ending too?

Mr. Whittington shot her a knowing glance. "The wheels of your busy mind have been turning, have they not? I imagine you have deduced why I came to Pleasant Creek."

Liz leaned forward. "Of course. You are looking for Priscilla."

His eyes moistened. "I did not even know about her until two years ago, and then it was too late. After searching high and low, I found she had passed away."

Liz clasped his hand while with the other, he pulled an enormous green paisley handkerchief from his pocket and dabbed his eyes. To discover a family member, only to lose her—Liz shared in his grief.

"Thank you." He stuffed the handkerchief back into his pocket. "For the sake of my mother, I assume, my father never told me about his past, nor did anyone else. I would not have discovered I had an older sister at all had I not decided to rid my attic of my pack-rat father's belongings. The cleaning people I hired brought down several old trunks. One contained letters Sally had written him while he was in England. You can imagine my reaction."

Liz exhaled. "I'm not sure I can." Her mother's Amish heritage had been surprise enough. Liz had no idea how she would have reacted to news of a sibling she'd never known.

"At first, my father's actions came as a terrible shock," he admitted. "One always believes one's parents are saints, not flesh and blood. However, I realized I might discover family members I never knew I had. Perhaps I was not alone in this world after all."

How well she knew that feeling. After her mother's death, Liz had yearned to belong to a family somehow, somewhere.

"Those letters provided hints about Sally's family. Using those, and talking to her kin, some of whom had left the Amish faith, I managed to track Sally's and Priscilla's journey to Indiana."

"Have you found any indication her descendants live here?"

He sighed. "Nothing substantial. I have not found any Hertzlers— Priscilla's adopted name—in local records. But Amish families rarely reported births, marriages, or deaths to the county. I have experienced great difficulty determining who belonged to what family."

"Few would want to discuss Priscilla with you." Liz recalled her own challenges in connecting personally with her Amish relatives. Mr. Whittington, with his odd clothes and British accent, would have even more.

"Not many Amish wish to discuss a church member's illicit love affair with an English man and the resulting child, even if it was several generations back." He sighed, then fixed a pleading gaze on Liz. "Since coming here, I have learned you not only found your Amish kin, but you are also a solver of mysteries. Am I too presumptuous in asking for your help? For I am sure you understand that my quest is not an idle one—it is a journey of the heart."

How could she do otherwise? "I would be glad to do what I can. Though that may be very little."

"Perhaps you could ask among your relatives if someone owns a similar tea set?" Mr. Whittington inquired hopefully. "Someone whose forebears passed it down?"

Gently rubbing the teacup's golden edge, Liz bit her lip. "A set this ornate would not be acceptable in many Amish congregations, and our local group is one of the more conservative."

"So I have come to realize." His chin dipped. "But for the sake of family might someone keep it? For the sake of love?"

How could she help him understand that the Amish cared deeply for their families, yet would shun them without hesitation if they defied the bishop's tenets?

Yet she could not stamp out his faint hopes. "Perhaps I could talk to my cousin Miriam. While a church member in good standing and strict in her own convictions, she would understand your search better than most Amish. And if any mention of a tea set has been made, she probably would have heard of it."

"Thank you." Mr. Whittington clasped her hands in his own. "I cannot tell you what this means to me."

He gave her Priscilla's birth date: April 5, 1920, which Sally had mentioned in one of her letters. "And I found the date of Priscilla's passing on a cemetery website. July 14, 2014. I visited that small cemetery in the southern part of the county. But no stone had been placed on her grave or any others, save a few small wooden markers with initials—a common custom among the Swiss Amish, I am told. Local families maintain that cemetery, so my inquiries were met with silence." His eyes moistened again.

Liz wrote down the dates. With difficulty, she escaped more thanks from him and returned to her apartment for a lunch of yogurt and fruit before the Brumpetts arrived. She probed her own mind regarding Priscilla and the tea set, though she doubted any results would surface.

As she'd told Mr. Whittington, she'd never heard anything resembling Priscilla's story at a quilting or any other gathering of Amish women. Even if they gossiped about such goings-on privately—which Liz doubted very much—they would not do so in the presence of an outsider. Besides, the scandal had taken place so long ago . . .

As for the tea set—her Amish relatives all used plain crockery, attractive in its own way, but nothing like this.

Or did they?

She now remembered little pigtailed Addie King the day Liz had helped after the Kings' burglary. The girl had asked Lydia if she and her friends could play with her dolly's teacups. Her mother had refused, quite sharply.

Uncharacteristic for Lydia, the doting mother of an only child. But then, she had suffered trauma and loss that day.

On the other hand, if Addie's tea set was everyday crockery, would she have to ask special permission to use it?

Liz, you're thinking too much. She tried to toss out her confused thoughts the way she tossed her banana peel.

Her mind, though, refused to back off. Perhaps Lydia had taken away Addie's set as a disciplinary measure. Or maybe the little girl's tea set had been destroyed during the burglary, and Lydia couldn't yet deal with her child's pain.

Or was the tea set a cherished secret to be concealed from other Amish church members, particularly critical family? A picture of Lydia's sharp-eyed mother-in-law prodded Liz's mind.

If Lydia did, in fact, possess Priscilla's tea set, she would hide it from family as well, so well that even the burglar had not found it.

But she might privately share it with her pigtailed daughter, who would delight in its butterflies and drink from the flowered cups, along with her faceless Amish dolls . . .

Liz shook herself. Asking about the presence of such unsanctioned possessions could make Lydia even less popular with her husband's family. Liz's cherished connections with her own relatives could be disrupted as well, especially if the bishop disapproved of her digging up a local family's dirt.

At the same time, should Mr. Whittington be condemned to a life without family?

As the doorbell chimed, Liz resolved to talk to Miriam later about her quandary. Perhaps her understanding cousin knew some tidbit of information that would help settle Liz's mind. Or maybe Miriam could supply direction in a situation that defied the rules.

Opening the door, she had never seen two women who looked more—or less—alike.

They possessed the same coloring, average height, and cute, chubby build. They had to be sisters and were probably around seventy. But one wore her hair in a silver, helmet-like cap and sported a flowery pantsuit probably visible several miles away, accessorized with sparkly stilettos and bag. The other woman wore a pastel dress with a lace collar, her hair in soft curls around her face.

"I'm Maxine Brumpett." The first woman's sharp blue eyes appraised Liz, then darted around the rotunda. "Are you sure you don't have any rooms on the first floor?" Her gaze fastened on the door to Liz's quarters.

"I'm sorry, Ms. Brumpett, but as we discussed on the phone, all guest rooms are on the second and third floors." Liz pointed to the staircase. "After you register, I'll be glad to help with your bags."

Maxine shrugged. "Well . . . I guess we've already paid for tonight. Where do I sign?" She filled out their paperwork.

The other woman held out a fragile hand. "I'm Marlene. What a lovely inn."

"Thank you." Liz's smile returned. *Well, one pleasant guest out of two isn't bad.*

Marlene added, "But I think it would look nicer if you painted the walls pink."

Sadie would probably agree with you there.

"Not a bright, horrid pink. Something soft and soothing. It would look so much better than this cream color."

What can I say? "I'll call the painters right away?" Liz ventured, "You'll be glad to know that you'll be staying in a room with pink walls, our Rose of Sharon Room."

"I hope to goodness the air-conditioning works." Maxine turned a wrathful eye on Liz.

Whew! "Uh, yes, it works quite well."

"I could not believe the last place we stayed." Maxine scowled. "Nothing but excuses when the central air broke down."

"I broke out in hives." Marlene's big blue eyes, fringed with long lashes, reminded Liz of a baby doll's.

Liz ended up lugging most of the bags upstairs by herself. When she asked Marlene to help haul her extra-large suitcase, the woman declined, citing back problems. Maxine complained for five minutes about the lack of staff, then finally aided Liz.

When Maxine inspected the room, though, the peppery sister's face broke into a smile. "What a beautiful quilt. Rose of Sharon pattern, isn't it? And antique lace on these shams. Such lovely flower prints on the wall."

Liz wanted to pump her fist. A kind remark at last.

"I don't know about the color on the walls, though." Marlene shook her head. "Is the pink a little too bright?"

"Gene Stratton-Porter!" Maxine, checking the antique bookshelf, found the old copy of *Freckles* Liz had bought at an estate sale. "She was my favorite author when I was a girl."

"I've enjoyed getting to know Stratton-Porter's works since I moved here," Liz said. "I try to keep Indiana authors' books throughout the inn."

After describing the inn's amenities, Liz went downstairs to prepare for coffee hour.

Mr. Whittington, do your magic. Please.

When he entered the sitting room, however, Maxine and Marlene nearly dropped their butterscotch bars.

Mr. Whittington still wore his Sunday morning Cat-in-the-Hat ensemble. But for unknown reasons, he'd changed his white shirt to a pink-and-purple jungle print.

Even Liz, now accustomed to his getups, wanted to close her eyes. Instead, she smiled weakly as she introduced him. "Mr. Cyrus Whittington, from Fort Wayne, is also a guest here at the inn."

"Good evening, ladies." Mr. Whittington raised his hat with his Cary Grant gesture. "My, Ms. Eckardt, you did not tell me you were expecting such charming guests. Are you twins?"

Liz had prayed for a miracle, and now she was witnessing it.

"No, but we're sisters." The steely-eyed woman simpered like a teen groupie. "I'm Maxine Brumpett, from Ohio."

"I'm Marlene Brumpett." Liz had noticed that Marlene usually moved with languid, my-back-hurts-but-I-never-complain grace. Now, however, she grabbed a teacup with one hand and, as if she were hostess, offered the wooden box containing teas with the other. "Would you care for a cup, Mr. Whittington?"

"Don't presume, Marlene." Her sister dazzled even Liz with her smile. "Mr. Whittington may like coffee." She held out a mug and the Longaberger basket of individual coffee pods.

"Er—I appreciate both." Though Liz knew British-y Mr. Whittington preferred tea, he made a gallant show of drinking the coffee Maxine prepared for him.

Though they incessantly sugar-and-creamed him through coffee hour, he seemed to enjoy swapping stories with both ladies.

He made chivalrous—but futile—efforts to include Liz in the conversation.

Normally, when guests relegated her to the roles of maid and wallpaper, Liz struggled a little with junior-high syndrome.

This afternoon, though, she gladly stayed in the background as the Brumpetts waged territorial war for Mr. Whittington's attention.

Any other observer would have sworn he enjoyed every minute of their company. But when Mr. Whittington rose and stretched, excusing himself to go exercise, Liz couldn't blame him for wanting to escape.

Maxine, however, saw his ruse as an opportunity for more togetherness. "Just the thing I need to lose those butterscotch bars. Let's walk around the lake."

"What a perfectly lovely idea." Fluttering her eyelashes, Marlene took Mr. Whittington's arm. "The doctor says I need to walk more, and what could be better for me, with such nice, strong support."

Maxine grasped his other arm, and before Liz could blink, the sisters had edged their victim to the four-season room and out the back door.

Liz watched the trio head toward the path that circled Jaynes Lake. The man probably could have outmaneuvered one of them. But without prior warning, even he was no match for their competitive one-two punch.

Had they perfected this dubious approach over the decades? Liz imagined the two ambushing high school dates, then unsuspecting middle-aged bachelors with good jobs and bank accounts.

Liz stirred a new pitcher of lemonade for their return, adding sliced lemons. Clucking her tongue, she wondered if, after several hours with the Brumpetts, Mr. Whittington might slip a little something extra from a private stash into his lemonade to soothe his frazzled nerves. She wouldn't blame him.

For herself, Liz would take deep breaths and count to ten thousand, for both the Brumpett women and Mr. Whittington were set to stay the entire week.

7

"Pssst. Ms. Eckardt."

Liz, who had just let Beans out, jumped at the sound of a male voice. But only for a split second. Mr. Whittington, white hair disheveled, gestured to Liz from the stairs.

"Sorry to startle you, my dear," he half whispered, drawing her into the sitting room. "But I wanted to let you know I shall not be taking breakfast here this morning."

She wasn't surprised by his boycott. "We certainly will miss you."

"I have an, er, early appointment."

His early appointment probably consisted of hiding behind a newspaper at Mama's. Or fleeing to England.

"Then I plan to visit a glass museum in Dunkirk." The old gentleman tugged the collar of his gold-and-blue vintage Nehru jacket. "I've heard it is one of the best collections in the area."

Liz said, "I've never driven over that way."

"I look forward to it. I found the opalescent stained glass factory in Kokomo fascinating." His eyes shone like his subject. "In the glassmaking process, workers there use the same furnaces and much of the equipment they did a century ago. Rooms there fairly burst with beautiful glass. They do blowing and molding at that factory too. In fact, I plan to revisit the Kokomo factory tomorrow. I cannot wait to see it again."

He paused. "Would you and your friends like to accompany me for their tour? It begins about half past ten. And I would love to take you all to lunch."

Now that the inn's air-conditioning worked, hot glassworks no longer sounded daunting. Liz always enjoyed exploring her still-new hometown and state.

The Brumpetts bumped her mind. She hedged, "Do you mean the Material Girls?"

"Yes, that is what I had in mind. Lovely ladies, all." He cast a hunted look through the open door toward the rotunda stairs. "But I am *positive* Miss Maxine and Miss Marlene have other plans."

"Indeed?" Liz found her voice mimicking his, her relief wrestling with guilt.

"However, if your young man would like to come, he is most welcome."

Liz's cheeks warmed. "My calendar is clear. I'm not sure who will be free, but I'll check."

"How kind of you." He lowered his voice another notch. "Perhaps. . . we might meet elsewhere? In your church parking lot?"

"That might work."

"Excellent. Many thanks." Mr. Whittington waved and hurried to the door, pausing to pat Beans, who was waiting outside at the threshold. Then the octogenarian rushed toward the parking lot faster than she'd thought possible.

As Beans entered, he eyed Liz, reminding her she'd left him standing outside.

"Sorry, guy." She petted him. "Guests come first, you know."

The bulldog ambled back to his rug and collapsed. But he still stared at Liz, as if sensing her inner controversy about Mr. Whittington's outing.

"The man has every right to invite whomever he wants, you know," Liz told Beans.

Her listener cocked his head, as if to say, "Are you sure?"

She dropped beside him, rubbing his back. "What could I do? I can't make my guests get along."

Beans closed his eyes. But with a low groan—his doggy version of a purr—Beans obligingly turned over so she could rub his stomach too.

"I can't pet you all morning. I have things to do."

"Such as make breakfast?" suggested a voice behind her.

Maxine. Liz pasted a smile on her face and stood. "Good morning. I hope you slept well?"

"I might have, if it hadn't been for all those roosters." Maxine glowered. "How many do they have in this town? Isn't there any way to shut them up?"

"I'm quite sure zoning laws prohibit keeping chickens in town. The ones you heard must live on farms near the town limits." *And sorry, I'm not going to ask my Amish friends to muzzle their roosters.* She summoned her hostess persona. "Which would you and Marlene prefer, omelets or pancakes?"

"Marlene likes pancakes, but make it omelets," Maxine said matter-of-factly. "I hate onions. But use lots of cheese. No American."

She walked to the sitting room and peered in. "No Mr. Whittington? Still asleep? Or is he already in the dining room?"

"No, he had an early appointment." What a wonderful word, "appointment." It covered a multitude of sins. Sort of.

Maxine's face fell. "But he's returning later?"

She looked so disappointed. Liz infused some warmth into her voice. "He said he'd be back sometime today."

Maxine exhaled. "I suppose I'd better wake up Marlene, or she'll sleep all morning."

Past seven, even? "Please help yourself to the beverage bar in the sitting room," Liz said. "I'll have omelets ready in a jiffy."

Maxine nodded and headed for the stairs. Liz started toward the kitchen.

"One more thing, Ms. Eckardt."

She halted, as if stopped in a school hallway by the principal. "Yes?"

"Are the eggs fresh?"

———— 〰〰〰〰〰〰〰〰〰 ————

The following morning, Liz had again spent breakfast with the two dragons—Maxine, who huffed and puffed scorching disapproval over everything, and Marlene, the seemingly sweet one who flapped continually about the gloomy day's effect on the dining room's color.

But when she and her friends arrived at the glassworks, she encountered a dragon of a different sort—a huge, century-old, 12-pot tank furnace. Could it be scarier than the dragons back at the inn? Liz held her breath as she strained to see inside its glowing gold and ruby maws. No, this old monster was much less frightening than the ones staying in her inn.

Workers pulled luminous globs of melted glass from the furnace and ran it to other employees, who used antique equipment to roll the globs into sheets.

"We have to get the glass to the right place in seconds, or it will crack later," their tour guide explained. "We also have to keep the furnaces burning day and night, just as they did a hundred years ago. Though the factory's hot this summer, it's nothing like what workers endured then, thanks to air-conditioning."

"Things get a little hot down at the town hall sometimes," joked Jackson, who had come with Liz, "but I think I'll stick to mayoring over this."

"I don't know how anyone can work within ten feet of that furnace," Caitlyn said.

"Glass holds the furnace's heat in its very heart. That's where it gets its glow," Mr. Whittington told her.

"How right you are, sir." Tom, the guide, didn't seem to mind the old gentleman's commentary. Tom directed them to a room full of large sheets of glass infused with swirling blends of every color imaginable. A historic wall, with signatures from almost every employee since the late 1800s, added to the charm of the glassworks.

"Opalescent stained glass," Tom said. "At the beginning, we mix compounds into the melt that produce various shades when the glass is annealed, or heated, then cooled slowly enough that it doesn't crack from the temperature change. We still use 'recipes' that are over a century old to color our glass. If an artist or company needs a specific color we don't usually offer, we will custom-mix the color they need."

"Gorgeous," Liz murmured.

The glassblowers, working in pairs, fascinated their group. Before the visitors' very eyes, little bubbles of glass morphed into exquisite works of art.

Mr. Whittington was right. The place presented an eclectic combination of modern plant, sooty-walled historical site, and glistening fairyland. It was well worth the visit.

They visited the gift shop afterward, where Mr. Whittington attracted odd looks, though his ensemble today was less vibrant than his others were wont to be. Along with his usual top hat and slippers, he wore a drab olive work shirt and shiny, pin-striped, polyester bell-bottoms.

He paused before a large, multicolored swirl of glass.

Liz joined him. "How exquisite. Another item for your collection?"

"Perhaps." Mr. Whittington changed his vantage point. "Can you see Indiana in this piece?"

What did he mean? She changed positions too, and took a second, long look. "I can."

Gilded stripes of green and yellow, paired with ovals of morning-glory blue and white, made her think of ripening cornfields under a late summer sky.

Liz read aloud the work's title on its tag: "Hoosier August."

If Mr. Whittington hadn't bought it, she would have. Instead, she contented herself with a small, intricate stained glass magnet.

As if the day hadn't already proved a delight, Mr. Whittington insisted on taking them to lunch at Hamminger House, a stately gas-boom mansion-turned-restaurant that boasted al fresco dining under a vine-covered portico and antique furnishings.

"You already paid our tour fees. We cannot allow you to pay for lunch," Liz objected.

"I certainly shall." Despite everyone's protests, Mr. Whittington persuaded the waiter to give him the bill and then the party went to the restaurant's gift shop.

Liz was enchanted by a set of Victorian velvet pincushions. These she insisted on purchasing herself.

After riding back to Pleasant Creek in Liz's Acura, they all thanked Mr. Whittington for a perfect day.

"It's a shame the others couldn't come." Caitlyn, in the backseat, was reexamining the blown-glass bead necklace she had bought. "Maybe we can take them some other time. It's a magical place."

Jackson agreed. "I've lived in this part of Indiana most of my life, but I had no idea that that glassworks existed."

While the others chatted, Liz drove the sunny road to the church parking lot, pondering her contradictory guest. Mr. Whittington must have purchased most of his wardrobe at the Salvation Army. She knew he drove his coupe around the county, searching for the cheapest gas. And he insisted on procuring free newspapers from fast-food restaurants by the interstate.

Yet he had paid for two full weeks at her inn. Today, he had bought several *objets d'art* that had cost plenty. He had also treated Liz and her friends like royalty.

A twinge of unease nudged her. No other guest had demonstrated such extreme generosity. Liz tried not to let her lawyer persona rule her attitudes, but such lavish givers sometimes concealed shady actions. Since Mr. Whittington's arrival, two Amish burglaries had taken place. Could he somehow have been involved?

He also could be lonely. No wife. No daughter. Liz reproached herself for her suspicious nature. *Maybe he is just a generous old sweetie.* She thought of his masterminding this outing without the Brumpett women and grinned. *A shrewd old sweetie.*

Mr. Whittington probably had devised more strategies to deal with the sisters. Sure enough, when she pulled into the church parking lot, he told her he would not be present for coffee hour. "I discovered a glass festival this week in a town about an hour's drive away. It has glassworks and a vintage car cruise Reg and I might enjoy." He began to lower the vintage convertible's roof.

"I've heard they have a quilting show too," Caitlyn said.

Mr. Whittington gestured toward his coupe. "Care to join me, Caitlyn? Just think of me as a nice grandpa with a great ride."

She chuckled. "I'd be delighted to be your honorary grand-daughter for the day. I'll just leave my car in the church parking lot." Turning to Liz and Jackson, Caitlyn urged, "Why don't you two meet us there?"

Liz teetered on the edge of temptation—a festival afternoon with the others? Or deep-cleaning the kitchen, possibly smothered by the Brumpetts?

One option sounded infinitely more pleasant than the other.

But she shook her head. "I've played enough. Besides, with the drive, I'd barely arrive at the festival before I'd have to return to the inn for coffee hour."

"I should get back to work too." Jackson sighed wistfully. "Fall orders at the store are piling up. I'm grateful for the business of course, but glass is so much more fascinating after this morning's tour."

Mr. Whittington and Caitlyn, her hair shining in the now brilliant sunlight, waved as they drove off in Reg.

"We're party poopers." Jackson grimaced.

"True." Liz sighed. "But I'll take innkeeping anytime over the corporate world."

The twinkle returned to his eyes. "At least we got to play hooky half a day. When you get the urge to do it again, let me know."

She grinned. "Will do. But right now, you've got a furniture store to run, and I've got an inn to keep."

His cell phone rang. With a sigh, Jackson clapped it to his ear. "Hey, Chief. What's up?"

The smile faded from his eyes as he listened.

Liz waited, holding her breath.

He hung up, his handsome face grim. "While the Sommer family was helping with church services on Sunday, the burglars struck again."

8

"I hope you don't mind my tagging along with you again," Liz told Mary Ann as they drove to the Wickeys' farm the next day. Mary Ann, an unofficial town representative when disaster struck, had loaded her sedan with disposable coolers of food contributed by the Material Girls. They planned to share it with the Wickeys and the Sommers.

"I always enjoy any time we can spend together—even this." Mary Ann sent a warm, penetrating glance Liz's way. "You're on the trail of something, aren't you?"

Liz shook her head. "I'd just like to know details from the other break-ins so I can settle a few things in my mind."

"Such as whether these criminals will attack your family next?"

"Something like that," Liz admitted. "But I have no intention of upsetting the Wickeys or the Sommers. They've been through enough."

"I know you won't. Actually, your presence might be a comfort to them."

Liz blinked. "Why?"

"They don't trust the police, but they know you have solved crimes." Mary Ann chuckled as she turned down the Wickeys' lane. "Not that they'd ever ask for your help. In their eyes, seeking justice smacks too much of taking revenge. But knowing that you, a proven sleuth, are concerned about their burglaries will mean something to our Amish neighbors."

If you say so. Even with Liz's own Amish heritage, would she ever understand the sect the way Mary Ann did?

A large, gray-haired woman wearing a pale-blue dress, white apron, and black Kapp waved at them from the farmhouse porch as Mary Ann stopped her sedan.

Liz loved the circus-colored array of zinnias, geraniums, and marigolds blooming in Mrs. Wickey's huge flower beds. While the Amish dressed in black and quiet pastels, they had no qualms about flashy flowers.

She helped Mary Ann carry a cooler to the porch, where her friend introduced her to Mrs. Huldah Wickey, her two daughters, a young new daughter-in-law, and several children.

"*Ja*, I have seen you at barn raisings," the elderly woman said in heavily accented English. "And at the wedding of Sarah and Isaac Borkholder."

They welcomed the food with big smiles and a chorus of "*Dänka.*" The matriarch directed the others to take the coolers to the kitchen.

"Though we have trouble, *Gött* has blessed us with good friends." Mrs. Wickey led them into her plain but spotless parlor and invited them to sit in the straight, cushionless chairs typical of this area's Amish. A preteen girl brought them glasses of lemonade.

Oh, for a fan. Even a paper one. The Amish, wearing flapping, long-sleeved dresses, didn't seem to notice the heat and humidity. But Liz knew she resembled a waterfall.

While Mary Ann carried on most of the conversation with Mrs. Wickey, Liz tried to ignore the heat and took mental notes. During this burglary, more damage had been done in the barn than in the house. The vandals had ravaged the kitchen and dumped out drawers, but in the barn, harnesses, bridles, and saddles had been slit, with feed and hay scattered everywhere. Worse, a buggy had been vandalized, and tools and a colt had been stolen.

"It was to be a wedding gift for our *Sön*, Laban, and his new *Braut*,"

Mrs. Wickey explained to Liz. She wiped away a tear with her apron. "For when they have their own *Valga*."

"Buggy," Mary Ann translated for Liz.

"But now the horse is gone. Will they find him? We do not know."

The pretty young wife, bringing the emptied coolers back to Mary Ann, dabbed at her own tears.

Horses are so important to these people. How sad. And what a way to start a marriage. Above all things, Liz had wanted to help Lydia. But the Wickeys' trials made her their ally as well.

She'd clenched her fists again—not an acceptable gesture in an Amish home. Liz straightened her fingers, puzzling over the Wickey and King incidents. Here, their barn had been targeted, whereas most of the damage done at the Kings had occurred inside their house. Glancing around the parlor and dining room, Liz saw no evidence of wall or floor damage as in the Kings' home. But then, the Wickey burglary had taken place four days before. Even in that small stretch of time, skilled Amish craftsmen might have restored the rooms to their original state.

Such differences might mean nothing. Still, Liz probed a little. "Your house is so pleasant. Mary Ann and I helped clean up at the Kings' home. Such destruction!" She described the men's efforts to fix the damage.

Mrs. Wickey clucked her tongue. "I heard. It was so much worse there. Poor Lydia."

Later, they visited the Sommers, victims of the most recent burglary, which had taken place sometime last Sunday. Mary Ann and Liz heard a similar tale. While their kitchen had been vandalized and some closets emptied, they had experienced a far worse barn invasion than home invasion. The family's large herd of dairy cows had been found wandering along various county roads the next morning. One had been hit by a semitrailer and killed.

"We are thankful we lost only one," Ezra Sommer told Mary Ann.

His four sons—particularly his eldest, a large, muscular young man with glinting blue eyes—didn't appear nearly as grateful as their father.

"No wonder they looked so mad. Gideon and his brothers probably spent the night running down those cows and bringing them home," Mary Ann said as they headed back to town.

She drove back faster than usual. "I just want to see my shop—all those pretty bolts of material in rows," she explained, "and all the notions in their little boxes, untouched by criminals like that."

Liz welcomed a return to her inn as well. Doing laundry washed away a little of the world's dirt. With Maxine and Marlene off to visit relatives until coffee hour, she accomplished more than she'd expected.

The sisters hadn't mentioned Mr. Whittington's absence at breakfast this morning. Perhaps, with his elusiveness, they'd given up any notion of trapping him.

Liz hoped he wouldn't make himself too scarce. Maybe, with the arrival of the Stinsons from Tennessee tomorrow, he'd feel shielded somewhat from the women's attentions.

All this, of course, hinged on the Stinsons' meshing with Mr. Whittington. But everyone loved the eccentric old man. They probably would too, once they grew accustomed to his getups.

But would they—could they mesh with the Brumpetts?

Worse, what if they were kindred spirits with the sisters?

Liz realized she was twisting a dishcloth into knots.

Chill, girl. Most of her guests were fun and interesting. She'd depend on the law of averages, promising herself that the Stinsons would be awesome people. She glanced at the big kitchen clock. Two hours until coffee hour.

Liz slapped a peanut butter and jelly sandwich together for a late lunch. As she ate, her thoughts circled back to what she'd seen and heard at the Wickey, Sommer, and King farms.

She had not wanted to become involved in investigating these burglaries. But that was before she'd talked to the victims and seen the devastation they suffered.

She'd really like to bounce a few thoughts off Chief Houghton . . . and she'd definitely like to hear any insights he might offer. Had he also wondered about Mr. Whittington's possible role in the break-ins? Though, considering the physical effort required for the rampages, the old gentleman would have had to have partners in crime.

Instead, maybe the chief had found a connection between Bingo Guy and the burglaries that he hadn't shared with her. Plus, she might glean other tidbits of information if he was in a good mood.

Hopefully his newborn granddaughter's colic had settled.

Sure enough, when she walked into his office, the chief's eyes seemed to have recovered some of their twinkle.

"Thought you'd show up soon. Heard you were out to see the Kings. And the Wickeys. And the Sommers."

She took the chair he indicated. "Mary Ann and I took food this morning."

"Of course, you did." His twinkle definitely had returned. "What do you want to know?"

Yes! Liz mentally scrolled through her list of questions.

"Did the Kings' barn look as bad as the others?"

"No, actually." The chief's graying brows lowered over his keen eyes. "Only a little hay and feed were scattered, and not much damage to harnesses and such. More stuff dumped out of toolboxes and cabinets there. Some loose boards had been yanked from the barn walls and the haymow floor."

"I saw boards pulled from the floors of the Kings' house too, and big holes in the walls. But that wasn't done in the other families' homes or barns." Liz watched the chief's fingers begin to drum on his desk. "Why do you think that was done at the Kings' place?"

"Not sure." He tilted his head. "What do you think?"

Who was gleaning info from whom? Liz said, "I think the burglars definitely were searching for something at the Kings' place. Were they at the other farms too? If they were, it wasn't as obvious." She shrugged. "Or maybe they found whatever they were looking for without tearing into walls and floors."

"Pretty much what I figured." The chief gulped coffee from his ancient Pleasant Creek Chamber of Commerce mug.

She shot a question back into his court. "I only saw the Wickey and Sommer farms after cleanup. Were their houses vandalized as badly as Lydia's?"

"No. Not sure why." Houghton topped off his coffee. "It was almost like the first burglary was aimed at what women value, and the last two at what men value."

"True." Liz had sensed that contrast, but hadn't put it into words. An odd difference. "Or the variations may go back to the intruders doing a search-and-destroy mission at the Kings' place, but focusing mostly on 'destroy' at the other two farms."

He beat her to her next question. "I asked the Kings if they owned anything worth ripping their house apart for. They said no, and I believe them." His forehead wrinkled. "Most folks around here know the Kings aren't rolling in money. I can think of lots of other places in the county that would generate a bigger take."

Unless that something valuable was Lydia's tea set. But if Mr. Whittington and/or his partners had been searching for it, why the unnecessary destruction? Aloud, Liz mused, "It does make me wonder if the burglars are from out of town. Did the other victims keep lots of cash around? Or some other valuables?"

"If they did, they're not telling me." Houghton sighed. "I try my best to get along with the Amish, and I think they respect me. But that doesn't mean they tell me what I need to know."

"You do walk a tightrope when it comes to solving their crimes." Liz knew the chief was equally committed to protecting both Amish and English, even when they didn't cooperate fully.

Houghton dropped his hands on his desk, a sign he'd soon end this interview. "Since you have family ties to the Amish community, you might hear something I don't. Keep me in the loop?"

"Of course." Liz stood. "I'll leave so you can get some work done. But I have to ask. Have you found out anything about the guy—or guys—Mary Ann, Naomi, and I saw?"

"For now, I'm assuming, like you, that we're dealing with one man. He hasn't surfaced again," the chief said, "though, with a good disguise, he could be walking the town square right now. We're keeping an eye out for someone with that stance. You watch out too." He stood and looked her in the eye. "Sooner or later, he'll make a mistake. Then we'll catch him and find out if he's a crackpot, a minor troublemaker, or somebody who's wrecking people's homes and livelihood."

Liz left the station believing that despite his eye rolls last week, the chief had taken her concern about Bingo Guy seriously. Plus, he'd made it clear that he would welcome her input about the burglaries.

On the way home, she scanned passersby, hoping to encounter the prowler again. After a few pedestrians returned her stares, however, she reminded herself to keep it subtle.

Arriving at the inn, Liz opened a cookie dough container and dropped snickerdoodles onto a cookie sheet for coffee hour.

Meanwhile, she wondered if Bingo Guy would appear again. What disguise would he use this time?

The phone rang.

"Olde Mansion Inn, Liz speaking."

At first she thought the "breather" from a few days ago had called again.

But a male voice, obviously altered, stabbed her ear. "Stay out of other people's business, Ms. Eckardt. Or else."

Click.

He sounded like a cross between an alien and Sean Connery. She almost laughed at the melodrama.

Instead, she noted the number. Hands shaking, she called the chief.

9

"That scuzzball," Sadie snarled as she trimmed seams with a vicious hand. "That sneaky, low-life *slime*! If we ever find that Bingo Guy, I'll hog-tie him and feed him to my cousin's pigs!"

Liz, passing out more quilting pieces to the other Material Girls, couldn't help laughing. "I don't know if he's the same man who called me, Sadie. Or even whether Bingo Guy is really bad news. If I figure out who he is, I'll sic you on him first."

Chief Houghton had been concerned enough to check the number she'd given him, which was a little disturbing. Yet his down-to-earth assurances also eased her mind.

And thank goodness the Material Girls were working on the pumpkin quilt tonight. There was nothing like a session in Sew Welcome's workroom to chase away the heebie-jeebies caused by nasty phone calls.

While they cut, pinned, sewed, and embroidered, Liz's friends alternately reassured her and metaphorically shook their fists at her caller. *Mister, when you harass one Material Girl, they will all come after you.*

Besides, Naomi had brought her famous cinnamon rolls, still warm from the oven, icing pooling on their tops. There wasn't much that could keep Liz down in the face of good friends and sweet treats.

Though her phone call and Bingo Guy tied for the top subject of discussion that evening, the burglaries came in a close second. As they rehashed details, Sadie declared Sew Welcome also had been the victim of a crime.

"Some thief took ten skeins of floss and embroidery needles from the rack." She steamed as if they were made of gold. "What is the matter with people? We hardly ever have problems like this."

In an effort to lighten Sadie's mood, Liz joked, "Maybe the same thief sneaked off with Sarah's furniture polish. She couldn't find it this morning."

They all chuckled, and Mary Ann said, "Now, Sadie, someone probably just forgot to pay."

"That customer probably will show up tomorrow, all embarrassed," Caitlyn predicted.

Mary Ann changed the subject to the wedding of Laban Wickey and Mercy Kirchhofer. She, Sadie, Opal, and Opal's husband, George, had attended the festivities.

"So sweet," Opal murmured as she cut more diamond-shaped pieces. "Mercy was a lovely little bride. So young, though. She's only sixteen."

"That's young even for the Amish," Sadie sniffed. "Why do you think her folks let her do it?"

"I heard the oldest Sommer boy wanted to court her and even managed to see her on the sly a few times." Mary Ann's ever-smiling face sobered. "He's the wildest of the *Rumschpringe* boys—and not a boy anymore. He's every bit of twenty-five and still causing his parents grief. When Laban, a responsible, kind young man, came courting, Mercy's parents were happy to give their blessing when the two wanted to marry."

So perhaps there had been competition between Laban Wickey of the colt loss and Gideon Sommer of the runaway cow hunt? Liz filed that information alongside countless other tidbits her fellow quilters had related during their sessions. They'd lived in the Pleasant Creek area their entire lives, so her friends sometimes filled in Liz's blanks when she couldn't find answers.

"I wonder if there was tension between the Sommers and the Wickeys because of that," Liz said, trying to keep her voice light. "Or between the Kings and either of the other two families for some other reason."

Opal pursed her lips. "I haven't heard of any problems between them."

Mary Ann nodded, then swung the group back to wedding chitchat: the new couple's gifts, new recipes tried out at the wedding feast, and the new crop of babies born since the last nuptial season.

Sadie, however, steered the conversation toward her new camper. "Only a few more days until our campout!"

Opal's lips tightened into a knot.

"It will be a nice getaway, Sadie," Liz said, hoping to diffuse any arguments before they began.

"Maybe with you gone, I'll *get away* from all this camping talk," Opal muttered. Glaring, she gathered up her personal supplies into a tote. "I'll see you all next week after the campout."

"See if I come to *your* birthday party," Sadie retorted.

"Who wants more cinnamon rolls?" Naomi whipped between the foes with a plateful. "Take one home for George, Opal? Plus one for you?"

Even Opal's ire had to subside. "They're his favorite. I guess I wouldn't mind another for the road, either."

Using her diplomatic voice, Mary Ann edged Opal out the door, while Naomi and Liz corralled Sadie.

At this point, no one was trying to talk Sadie out of her plans.

Why should we? It's her birthday. Liz watched her friend's eyes shine as she talked about her camper. *For Sadie, I think this is a dream come true.*

Caitlyn asked, "What kind of cake do you want for your birthday?"

"S'mores cake—what else?" Sadie licked her lips.

Liz was sorry to see Opal leave early, but the atmosphere relaxed, and they achieved their goal for tonight's session. The gilt-edged pumpkin patch was taking shape, and Liz and the others high-fived over their accomplishment.

"This quilt might not even make it to the festival," Caitlyn kidded. "I might just buy it for me!"

After cleanup and good-byes, Liz had just unlocked her apartment door when Mr. Whittington walked into the rotunda, carrying bags.

Liz readied for his usual show-and-tell, as Mr. Whittington had been adding to his collection daily—marbles, small sculptures, dishes, and knickknacks. Once, he'd showed her Venetian foil glass beads, with their exquisite interworking of colored, gold, and silver foil. A day later, he'd purchased the ugliest multicolored glass elephant she'd ever seen.

"Want to see what I found today?" Without waiting for an answer, Mr. Whittington unwrapped two carefully padded lumps.

Canning jars. Not the most exciting thing he'd brought back from his quests.

He didn't seem to notice her lack of enthusiasm. "You're familiar with Ball jars and the Ball family, who made them in Muncie? I went to Minnetrista, a center where the old Ball home used to stand. Had the good fortune to hit a Midwest Fruit Jar Club event," he crowed. "I have been looking for these for a long time."

"Congratulations." The man was beaming as if he'd unearthed diamonds. She had to smile.

"But that's not all." He unwrapped a small, padded packet. "I met a chap who was willing to sell me these."

She stared.

Eyeballs stared back. A blue pair and a brown pair.

Her mouth wobbled.

"Prosthetics. Wonderful German workmanship, all from the late 1800s." He glowed. "How lucky can one get?"

After informing her that he was coming to breakfast tomorrow, Mr. Whittington ascended the stairs, whistling.

Liz entered her quarters and locked the door.

No landline here to be called by unknown perverts. No pink camo campers, quarreling friends, fussy guests, or fake eyeballs. Just her nice, normal apartment. If only she could take refuge here for a few days . . . Mr. Whittington's presence at breakfast tomorrow would set off plenty of sister-versus-sister fireworks.

But not enough to burn down the inn, she hoped.

Liz could put out relational fires for a few more days. Then the Brumpetts were off to Michigan.

Cuddling her favorite pillow, Liz read a mystery novel until she fell asleep.

She dreamed Maxine and Marlene were witches with glass eyes. They waved magic wands, turning the Olde Mansion Inn into an enormous pink camo camper with a matching landline phone that never stopped ringing.

———————————

Liz had learned during the past few days that adding a few extra niceties sometimes helped placate the Brumpetts.

Sometimes.

So with the fragrance of ham, cheese, and egg casserole wafting throughout the inn, Liz set one end of the dining room's big mahogany table with antique linen place mats and napkins, a mix of crystal glasses, and the floral china she had found at Harvey's. The soft shade of colonial blue brought out the color of the darker walls, both emphasizing the room's patterned tin ceiling, lavish woodwork, and lead glass chandelier.

Liz added a big crystal vase of Queen Ann's lace she'd gathered near the lake and paused to absorb the ambience. Was this her favorite room? She never could make up her mind.

Though Marlene couldn't tolerate the place mats Liz had used one other morning, she hadn't yet found fault with the dining room's overall color scheme.

Besides, the Brumpetts' eating in the dining room, rather than the breakfast nook, gave Liz some space.

"Good morning, Liz."

Mr. Whittington had started calling her by her first name, though she couldn't bring herself to call him Cyrus. The smile and tip of his top hat made Liz realize how much she'd missed him the past several mornings. He carried a beige box he set on a small table near the door.

Mr. Whittington sniffed appreciatively. "Something smells delightful."

"I hope you enjoy it." She patted the gingham-cozied teapot. "Would you care for a cup now or later?"

As she suspected, the old gentleman welcomed a cup "until the others come." Chatting as she zipped in and out, Liz noted that he'd chosen a checked shirt and striped bow tie whose blues sort of matched. And a pair of pants that actually might have been made during the most recent decade.

He waggled a conspiratorial finger. "I do apologize, but I invited a guest to breakfast and neglected to tell you. I shall be glad to pay extra—"

"Not necessary, and no problem at all. An extra guest will keep me from eating too many leftovers."

Liz brought another place setting to the spot beside him. She easily made room for his . . . friend? Date? But if that guest were a lady, would the Brumpetts behave?

Right.

"Mr. Whittington! How delightful to see you." Maxine, wearing a neon-flowered muumuu, swept into the room, zeroing in on the chair beside him like a colorful missile.

But Marlene, with her deceptively languid gait, beat her to it. "Would you pour me some coffee, Liz?" She sighed. "I'm sorry, but my back hurts too much to stand up again."

Liz turned to the buffet, but Mr. Whittington took Marlene's cup. "Allow me the honor." He carried his and hers to the buffet, then addressed Maxine, who had turned all the colors of her dress. "May I also pour you a cup, Miss Maxine? Cream and sugar, ladies?"

Still flustered, Maxine nodded, glowering at her sister. Mr. Whittington took a cup from the place setting across from him.

Marlene smiled a slow catlike smile.

Score one for her, zero for Maxine. Liz busied herself arranging pastries and fruit.

He filled the cups from the carafe, added cream and sugar, and set one for Maxine beside Marlene—then set his tea across the table.

"Morning, everybody." Sadie, wearing a sundress that made her look twenty years younger, bounced through the door.

"Good morning, Miss Sadie." Mr. Whittington pulled out the chair beside him. "So glad you could come today."

Liz left under the pretense of checking on the casserole. She was really trying to get her emotions under control.

She'd said the inn wouldn't burn down, hadn't she? She could only hope she was right.

Liz grabbed hot pads and yanked the oven door open. What *was* the man thinking? If he'd wanted to ask Sadie to breakfast, why had he invited her here?

She *so* did not want to return to the dining room. But the casserole, light brown and bubbling, was done.

Five minutes. Could she spend five minutes serving, pouring coffee and tea, agreeing with everything everyone said?

Liz shuddered, then brightened. Sarah had just arrived. She could send Sarah to serve instead.

Liz's inner critic pointed a stern finger. *It's your job to manage guests. Are you an innkeeper or a mouse?*

She placed the casserole in a basket, took a deep breath, and marched back into the dining room.

Sadie was telling her latest lame joke. Mr. Whittington laughed delightedly. Liz thought the Brumpetts looked exactly alike when they wore matching scowls. They barely reacted to Liz's serving them.

Were they too mad even to complain?

Liz did her job and returned to the kitchen, hoping they'd finish quickly. A few minutes later, however, Sadie called to her.

"Liz, come here and see this!"

Blast. She sidled back into the dining room, where Sadie had opened Mr. Whittington's beige box. Her friend pointed to the swirls of green, gold, blue, and white glass, edged with gold. *Hoosier August.*

"Isn't it perfect?" Sadie beamed. "Just like the cornfields on my farm."

The Brumpetts sat stiff and mute as twin totem poles, their plates mostly untouched.

The glass sculpture *was* perfect for Sadie.

"It's lovely," Liz managed to say. She turned to the others. "May I warm your coffee, ladies?"

"Actually, I must be going." Maxine stood. "I have plans for today and won't be back for coffee hour."

"I'm not feeling well, I'm afraid." Marlene moved stiffly, as if in pain. "Count me out too." In spite of her words, she beat Maxine to the door. Both disappeared within seconds.

Liz picked up the casserole dish and took it to the kitchen. Slowly, she returned to the dining room and poured herself a cup of coffee, wishing she could shoot it directly into her veins.

"I suppose," Mr. Whittington said from behind her, "that was rather a beastly thing to do."

She turned to face him. If the Brumpetts wore look-alike frowns, he and Sadie sported twin grins and sparkling eyes.

You two are a dangerous combination. Liz tried, unsuccessfully, to hide her chuckle. "It certainly was. I take it you planned this little scenario?"

"Indeed we did." Sadie imitated his accent.

Liz clucked her tongue at the conspirators. "What do you two have to say for yourselves?"

"Call me a desperate man." Mr. Whittington sighed deeply, covering his heart. "If I could have communicated my lack of . . . interest in a more subtle way, I would have."

"Some people have to be hit with a two-by-four," Sadie said, crossing her arms. "Otherwise they don't get it."

"You're right," Liz admitted.

"Why should I hide like a hunted convict when I wish to enjoy this lovely inn and all it offers?" Mr. Whittington's eyes still twinkled, but he set his jaw. "When I encounter the ladies again, I shall be cordial and polite. But I refuse to bow to cave-woman tactics."

Apparently, the old gentleman's cloak of courtesy covered a little steel.

He inclined his head to Liz. "Thank you again for a wonderful breakfast." He turned to Sadie with a similar bow. "Ready for a drive with Reg?"

"Rarin' to go." She ran her fingers over *Hoosier August*, her snapping blue eyes suddenly gentle. "Thanks again for this beautiful gift, Cyrus. Let's drop it off at Sew Welcome before we leave."

"I'll do it for you," Liz offered. While Mr. Whittington would try to maintain civility, she wouldn't bet on the Brumpetts being able to do the same if their paths crossed.

She edged Sadie and Mr. Whittington out the back door instead, then watched them walk arm in arm to the parking lot.

Obviously, not all their charade had been staged.

How sweet.

How complicated.

But Liz wouldn't even think about that. Before she began breakfast cleanup, she dropped *Hoosier August* by Sew Welcome. Then she started upstairs to touch base with Sarah about the Amish Room, where today's new arrivals would stay.

At the top of the stairs, Liz heard a muffled scream.

Sarah.

Liz charged down the hall toward Mr. Whittington's room. Was it Bingo Guy? Or whoever was burgling Amish families?

Actually, it was Mr. Whittington's four glass eyeballs.

Sarah already had calmed down, but her face turned fiery red. "I am sorry, Ms. Eckardt." She pointed to Mr. Whittington's new additions. "Those things startled me, and—"

"What's going on?"

Maxine, always on patrol, should have been a policewoman.

"Nothing, Maxine. Everything's fine." Liz explained, then gently tried to back the woman out of Mr. Whittington's room.

"Eyeballs yet." Maxine rolled her own. "And look at that horrid elephant. He paid money for those? The man's crazy." She returned to the Rose of Sharon Room, nose in the air.

Liz hid a smile. Perhaps this incident, plus the earlier theatrics, might prove more effective than she'd thought.

She settled Sarah back into her cleaning routine and was contemplating her next move when Beans barked.

That was odd. Unlike most dogs, Beans never barked at mail carriers, UPS trucks, or repairmen. After eating breakfast, he usually remained comatose until he heard the can opener again.

Liz descended to find the bulldog actually standing by the front door.

Beans bared his teeth, and a low growl rumbled in his chest.

"What's the matter, boy?" If Sadie were here, this abnormal display of energy might result in an emergency visit to the vet.

He didn't growl or bark again, and he dropped back onto his rug. But his eyes remained open, and his ears were alert. Liz peered out a front window.

No one there. Only a small package.

She stepped cautiously outside. The package had her name and address on it. No return address.

Should she check with Chief Houghton before opening it?

Inside the door, a snore rent the morning air, growing louder every moment.

Beans certainly didn't appear concerned anymore.

Liz brought the package inside, slit its brown paper, and opened it.

Inside, a few glass slivers lay scattered atop wadded newspaper. A personal package, after all? But whatever had been sent was broken.

Carefully, to avoid cutting herself, she unwrapped the newspaper.

Fragments of an elegant teacup nested in the packing, tiny fragments as if the cup had not been broken so much as crushed.

She salvaged a few larger shards. Light colonial blue and white floral.

The cup was from her new tea set.

Liz caught her breath.

A small, typewritten note was with the cup.

I'm watching you. Stay out of my way.

10

"I really don't like this." Chief Houghton took pictures of the crushed teacup and the whole one Liz had brought from her cupboard.

"Doesn't exactly give me warm fuzzies, either." Liz tried to laugh.

"Looks like the same kind, all right." His fingers drummed on Liz's dining room table. "You're sure this teacup didn't come from your personal set?"

"Positive, though it matches mine." She'd been shaky when she counted her teacups, but none were missing. "How did this person know which dishes I use? Do you think someone's been looking in my windows?" She couldn't help glancing through the tall windows she loved.

"Possibly." Houghton examined the crushed teacup with gloved hands, his eyebrows lowered. "Glad you didn't handle it much. Who knows? They may have mixed something nasty into this dust." He began enclosing the box in a heavy plastic bag. "Better wash your hands thoroughly."

After she complied, he asked, "Could we go somewhere more private to talk?"

Liz directed Houghton, carrying the box, to the library, then shut the door behind them. "I only use those dishes when serving guests at breakfast, when it's broad daylight. I would think someone would have spotted a Peeping Tom."

"Who all knew you use these dishes?" The chief poised his phone to take notes.

"Um, well, all the guests: Mr. Whi—Cyrus Whittington—"

"Is that the old guy who wears a top hat around town?"

She chuckled. "Quite a sight, isn't he?"

"Well, if somebody's trying to hide something, they usually don't try to stand out like he does."

A point in his favor. Mr. Whittington also had been open with Liz, even sought her help to find Priscilla's tea set and its owner.

"Where's he from?"

"He just moved to Fort Wayne, but his house isn't ready yet. So he's staying here and giving himself a historical tour of Indiana's glass industry."

Liz counted on her fingers, "Then there are Maxine and Marlene Brumpett from Ohio, Richard and Sandra Fremont from Baltimore, and Tony Lanham from Michigan." She winced at the memory of Sadie practically running the poor bulldog lover out of the inn.

"Anyone else?"

"Well, Sadie ate breakfast here this morning. And Sarah, of course."

Houghton dipped his head so his gaze locked onto hers. "Anybody in that bunch mad at you? Mad enough to do this?" Using a probe, he poked at the layer of ground-up china in the bottom of the box.

Her throat constricted. "I'm not exactly Maxine and Marlene's favorite, but I get the feeling they don't like much of anyone. I seemed to click with the others. Though you never know with guests . . ."

She and Houghton had been fooled more than once by past guests. Liz shook off a shiver. She couldn't let paranoia spoil her hospitality.

"I don't think Sadie or Sarah have it in for me either."

"Not unless they've been fooling us for a while." He grinned, then his smile faded to seriousness again. "You bought these at the antiques store downtown, right? So it's not like somebody could go to Walmart and buy 'em."

"No. They're seventy-five years old. A person probably would have to search for them on the Internet—" She blanched. "Or buy them at

Harvey's. He had three extra place settings he'd gotten from an estate sale that I didn't purchase."

Houghton said sharply, "Was anyone with you when you bought the dishes?"

"No." She'd stopped by the antiques store on impulse and found the perfect pattern the day she'd gone to the farmer's market to buy fruit.

Liz's heartbeat throbbed in her ears. "That was the day I noticed the pigeon-toed businessman at the stoplight. You know, the one who might use disguises."

Houghton's eyes glinted. "Did you see him in Harvey's too?"

She pressed her forehead harder. "I didn't notice because I was trying to decide whether the china's color would match my dining room. There were people there, I know. A mother with a little girl, because she warned her not to touch anything. But I can't recall . . ."

"Don't worry about it. I'll talk to Harvey. Don't know if he'll remember everyone who walked through the door, but if this guy bought something with a charge card, we'll nail him fast."

"I'll go back to the store too." Liz bit her lip. "Maybe being there will jog my memory."

He patted her shoulder. "Don't be hard on yourself. You remember details better than anyone I know." He snorted. "Some people couldn't remember where they parked their cars if they painted 'em pink and purple."

Um . . . She wouldn't tell him how long she had searched for hers the last time she went to a mall in Fort Wayne.

The chief picked up the box with its shattered cup. "I doubt we can recover fingerprints from this, but you never know."

She frowned, tired of being on edge. "If he calls again, I'll blow a whistle into the phone."

The chief winced. "That might make him meaner. Just hang up.

After you take note of his number." A frown creased his face. "Though the numbers you've given me belonged to a disposable phone."

Surprise, surprise. Liz sighed. "I still haven't cleaned up breakfast, so I'd better take care of that. But I'll go by Harvey's later today."

He hesitated. "It's okay if you stop by once, but don't delve too deep. Then stay away from the place. Stay clear of the burglary victims too, or anything associated with them."

Seriously? She crossed her arms. "You think that has something to do with this?"

"Not sure. But local fame has followed you." His smile looked like a grimace. "Not that all the bad stuff going on is local. Your past involvement with solving crimes could easily have leaked to an outsider if he has some personal connection here. Bottom line, he probably knows you've helped put people in jail. People like him."

"Why would he think I'm on his trail, though? How does he even know he's on my radar?"

Now the chief counted on his fingers. "You've been at all the burglary sites, asking questions. You've talked with me a few times. You may have seen one of the guys involved when he didn't want to be seen. That's enough to make perps really nervous—which is why he or they pulled this little stunt."

"What should I do? Act like he's scared me off?" Liz asked.

Houghton's scowl deepened. "We'd better talk only by phone for a while. That might make him focus less on you. Hopefully we'll learn more before the burglar or burglars strike again."

"Oh, I hope they don't." Lydia's ravaged young face floated through Liz's mind. Mrs. Wickey's eyes full of pain. Ezra Sommer trying to count his loss as a blessing.

"Same here. Who knows? Maybe Harvey will identify this guy, he'll confess to the burglaries, and we'll clean up this mess in one afternoon."

A smile tugged at her mouth. "That would be nice. Then Mary Ann could make us a bunch of pies, and we could celebrate tonight."

"I'd vote for that." His genuine grin broke through, then retreated. "Until then, lay low. We'll keep an eye on you. Let me know if anything out of the ordinary happens, no matter how small and insignificant it may seem."

The chief hadn't yet driven away when Maxine popped up like a blister. She called from the stairway, "What were the police doing here?"

At least, she hadn't barged in on them in the library. Liz said carefully, "Stan's a good friend. He heard someone played a prank on me and dropped by to make sure that was all it was."

Her guest's X-ray eyes did not make this deliberate understatement easy, but apparently Liz pulled it off. Maxine sputtered, "With all the burglaries going on, I'd think a public servant would have better things to do."

She flounced back to her room.

Just a few more days till the Brumpetts leave. Liz looked at her watch, willing the time to move faster.

She poured her frustrations into cleaning the kitchen and pantry. Then after a gulped lunch of reheated soup, Liz walked downtown—one of her favorite places.

At least, it had been. Lately the town square made her edgy. It seemed she'd sprouted a dozen antennae that probed her surroundings, whether she wanted them to or not.

Despite the heat, the town square looked appealing, with big pots of miniature sunflowers, blue verbena, and white petunias brightening the streets. People shopped and stopped to chat. Children shrieked with laughter as they played under their parents' watchful eyes.

What had she expected? A black-cloaked villain skulking behind the clock tower?

She entered the antiques store, old sleigh bells jingling above the door as she stepped inside. Harvey, working with a customer, greeted her with a nervous smile.

Chief Houghton probably had already paid the shopkeeper a visit. She wandered the quaint little shop, ostensibly admiring lace-edged linens while examining every shelf and peering into every corner. Yet no memories of other shoppers from her last visit surfaced.

After Harvey's customer paid and left, the store's owner approached her, though his expression said he'd rather not. Harvey cleared his throat. "Anything I can help you with, Liz?"

"No, just enjoying your shop."

Harvey lowered his voice. "I hope you don't mind, but when Chief Houghton came in here this morning, asking questions about who shopped here last Wednesday, I had to tell him you were one of my customers." His nose twitched, and he reminded Liz of a rabbit. "He certainly didn't think you'd done anything wrong—"

"Of course you had to tell him." She poured as much reassurance into her smile as she could.

He exhaled, visibly relieved. "I knew you'd understand." Harvey's forehead furrowed. "He didn't say why he wanted to know, just requested a list of who came into the shop."

"Anybody I would know?" Liz asked, hoping her voice sounded casual. Actually, she hoped he'd inform her about customers she *didn't* know.

But Harvey didn't rise to the bait. "I'm sorry, Liz, but the chief told me to keep quiet about Wednesday. I've probably said too much already."

He skittered to the back room.

For a few minutes, Liz tried to regain her focus, to let the old toys in the children's section tell her the story of who had wandered the aisles then. But even the adorable Kewpie dolls kept their secrets.

She left, letting the shop's door bang a little louder than usual. She appreciated Houghton's keeping her freaky package under wraps, but he could have given Harvey a little leeway. He could have allowed the antique dealer to share what he knew with Liz alone.

Liz strode the sidewalk, too annoyed to notice her surroundings until Jackson's voice said, "Okay, today you *really* need ice cream."

She glanced sideways at his quicksilver grin and exhaled. "You're so right."

They walked to the ice cream stand, where Liz ordered homemade persimmon-cream-cheese ice cream drizzled with caramel and covered with whipped cream and pecans.

"Double dip," Jackson added, "or triple. Liz needs *serious* ice cream."

"Double." Liz shook her head at him, but didn't mind that he'd talked her out of the single dip she always ordered.

So she wouldn't feel bad, he said, Jackson ordered a double-scoop "To Die For Fudge Sundae."

They sat on a bench near the clock tower, gobbling ice cream like ten-year-olds. It was a pleasant change for someone who had been feeling like a hundred.

"Ice cream is one of God's greatest gifts to humanity," Jackson intoned, waving his plastic spoon. "It will brighten a bad day at the office, sweeten a relationship gone sour—" He lowered his voice. "And even negate the effects of creepy packages of crushed china cups."

She stared. "How did you know about my package?"

"Shh." He put a finger to his lips. "Chief told me."

He'd told Jackson, yet Harvey couldn't tell her anything? As Liz's stare morphed to a glare, he added, "I am the mayor around here, you know."

"I know."

"It's not like I looked in your windows."

She shivered, even as her hackles rose again.

His eyebrows did too.

"I'm sorry I'm so touchy." She took an extra-large bite and instantly regretted it when her head throbbed. "This week has been a bear. And it's maddening to be part of a case, yet forced to step back from it."

"Confusing," Jackson agreed. "Sure you don't need another dip?"

"No!" If she ate triple-dip sundaes during every frustrating week, she'd weigh as much as the clock tower.

Jackson's teasing dwindled to a respectful silence.

She sighed. "I know the chief is trying to keep me safe."

"He is. Whoever sent this has a nasty streak, Liz." There was no trace of a smile in Jackson's face now. "The chief also told me about the package because he's short of officers right now. He hoped I could check in with you on a regular basis."

Something else to cramp her style?

But at the concern on Jackson's face, she couldn't cling to her sulk. "What did you have in mind?"

"Maybe I could call you every morning and every night?" Jackson suggested. "And occasionally drop in for coffee?"

"Don't forget ice cream patrol." She licked the last bit of caramel from her spoon.

He raised a hand in a mock salute. "Never!"

She smiled. "Thanks, Jackson. It's not like you don't have enough to do already."

"My pleasure."

The warmth in his voice made her glance at her watch. "I have guests coming! I'd better get back to the inn."

"Ice cream patrol isn't complete until I've brought you to your door." Jackson kept her laughing as they walked, bowing with a flourish before he headed back to his store.

Maybe "stepping back" wasn't going to be so bad. She smiled as she watched his tall, athletic figure stride away.

Still, Liz continued to scan the street, as she had every minute downtown with Jackson. No sign of Bingo Guy today. That didn't mean he wouldn't show up tomorrow, disguising everything but his stance.

Chief Houghton hadn't left her much choice about taking a step back.

But if she kept her eyes open, maybe she could still move this case forward.

11

Maxine and Marlene failed to show for breakfast the next morning. Mr. Whittington aimed apologetic glances Liz's way.

He appeared to try to make amends by charming Megan and Kyle Stinson, Liz's thirty-something guests from Tennessee.

"Y'all have made us feel right at home," Kyle Stinson, a brawny, friendly man, helped himself to three more biscuits and a mound of bacon.

His petite blonde wife nodded. "I can't wait to shop downtown. And to see Amish country!"

If she hadn't dragged her husband away, Liz mused, would Kyle have started raiding the refrigerator? That guy could eat.

Mr. Whittington remained. Like a schoolboy, he sidled up to her. "Ms. Eckardt, I do want to express how very sorry I am that I offended the Brumpetts."

"Whether they eat here or not is their choice."

"Nevertheless, I feel I should pour oil on their troubled waters. Would you aid me in doing so?"

Um . . . "Certainly." Liz pasted a smile on her face.

"I had hoped we could use my tea set during coffee hour today."

A unique idea. Would the Brumpetts like it? Would they even show up?

Mr. Whittington must have sensed Liz's doubts. "I thought I would show the set to Ms. Maxine and Ms. Marlene this morning and issue a special invitation with your help. I ordered espresso and English treats from Naomi for the occasion."

"Wonderful!" Liz didn't mind a break from baking. And perhaps, in sharing the exquisite little-girl tea set, tensions might ease among her guests.

"Perhaps we should take care of that task immediately—before we convince ourselves otherwise." Mr. Whittington stood and headed upstairs.

For an eighty-year-old man, he moved fast. Liz trailed after him. "What am I supposed to do?"

"Agree with everything I say, of course. And if they attack, defend me with your life."

She chuckled.

He retrieved the tea set from his room and rapped on the sisters' door.

Both Maxine and Marlene answered. Their faces froze.

Until they saw the tea set.

"How adorable!"

"Where did you find this?"

"Such a sweet little teapot!"

Liz feared the Brumpetts would think he was presenting it to them as a peace offering. But when Mr. Whittington told them it had belonged to his late daughter, their eyes softened with understanding, and both expressed sympathy.

"I had hoped," the octogenarian said with exactly the right touch of pathos, "that in Sherry's honor, you would join us and the other guests at a special coffee hour today, using her tea set."

"What a lovely idea." Marlene bestowed a winsome smile on him. "I will come."

Even Maxine's ire dissolved like a sugar cube in hot tea. By the time Liz and Mr. Whittington retreated, the more irascible woman also had agreed to attend.

All without Liz saying a word. The man was a master at managing human nature.

Or was he a manipulator? He had used the tea set—and his late daughter—quite effectively . . .

Mr. Whittington possessed an uncanny ability to read Liz's mind. As he handed the tea set over to Liz, he whispered, "Perhaps you thought my mention of Sherry laying it on a bit thick?"

"Well . . . yes."

"I assure you, if she were present, she would be holding her sides, laughing."

If Sherry had been anything like her father, Liz could easily believe that.

As Liz worked that morning, her thoughts returned to Mr. Whittington's request that she help him find his relations. She resolved to visit Miriam, who might know some tidbit of information that would help settle Liz's mind about his and Lydia's possible kinship. Or maybe Miriam could supply direction in a situation that defied the rules.

Later, however, when Liz and her cousin rocked on her front porch, Miriam shook her head. "I know very little about Lydia and Dale. He and Philip disagree on many issues, so we are not close."

Blast. Remembering the decorative star on Dale's barn, Liz could imagine Miriam's traditionalist husband clashing with the younger man.

"I do remember a few details about Lydia's family, though. Lydia's maiden name was Esh. Her mother, who was friends with my mother, mentioned Glicks somewhere in the family tree. But that is all I know." She grimaced. "That might not be at all helpful, as Glick is a very common name in our county. I have not the faintest idea which family might be related to her. You would have to ask Lydia herself."

Liz shook her head. "With no proof of her kinship with Priscilla, I don't think that's an option."

"No, it is not." Miriam paused. "Even with proof, she may not welcome kinship with Mr. Whittington. Do you think he's faced that possibility?"

"I hope he's considered it." Lydia might be familiar with Priscilla's illegitimate background, but dislike its coming to light.

Or the information might shock her, as it had him.

Liz fought a sinking sensation. She'd agreed to help Mr. Whittington because he desired family, as she had. She only hoped that should he succeed in finding his Amish relatives, the discovery would prove positive rather than negative, for all involved.

After a hug good-bye, Liz headed back to town, musing about her next move.

Since Mr. Whittington was supplying refreshments for coffee hour today, she had time to run to the courthouse to dig through public records. As she drove, Liz let a trickle of optimism water her thoughts. She'd done local research more than once in the past. With that experience, she might succeed where Mr. Whittington had failed.

And perhaps, Lydia and Dale—young and more open-minded than most Amish in the area—might consider befriending Mr. Whittington if they turned out to be family. Tired of their parents' criticisms, they might welcome a friendly elderly relative like him.

Liz didn't place much confidence in either possibility, but why not hope for the best?

The pleasant but inquisitive secretary welcomed her to the county clerk's office. When Liz asked for birth records from the first half of the twentieth century, the woman said, "You're the second person this afternoon to ask for those. The other lady still has them, I believe. Let's see if she's done."

The secretary took Liz back to the familiar musty room that

housed county records. A chic, dark-haired young woman sat at a table cluttered with black books full of faded, old-fashioned handwriting. Intent on her work, she did not appear to hear their arrival.

The clerk said, "Miss, are you finished with the 1900s birth records yet?"

The girl jumped. At the sight of Liz, her annoyed gaze froze, then flamed.

The secretary suggested, "Ms. Eckardt also needs to use them. Perhaps you could share the books—"

But the researcher had grabbed her designer bag. She brushed past them without a word.

"What in the world?" The clerk stared after the young woman as she strode past the counter and hurried into the hallway toward the nearest exit.

Liz rushed after her unexpected quarry, who dashed out a side door. Liz plunged after her, only to scan the manicured courthouse lawn in vain. Liz circled the building, hoping to catch another glimpse of the stranger who had shot her such a hostile glance.

No sign of her.

Questions assailed Liz as she paused outside the courthouse's front door to catch her breath. Who was the girl? Had she found the information for which she was looking? If she had something to hide, her overreaction toward Liz advertised rather than concealed her secret.

Was it a secret that connected with Liz's quest? Maybe Liz's fellow researcher had even tracked a link between Lydia and Mr. Whittington's half sister, Priscilla.

As Liz reentered the courthouse, she prepared herself to answer the curious secretary's questions. No, she'd never met that person before. She had no idea why the stranger had seemed hostile. Yes, Liz still wanted to do research, and no, she didn't need help.

After fluttering around Liz a few more minutes, the secretary returned to her desk.

The wooden chairs in the records room were hard and squeaky as ever, the big books dusty and full of illegible handwriting. *How I wish our county would put records online!*

But she wouldn't let a little grunt work get her down.

First, Liz checked birth records and found that Lydia's parents, though old-school, had submitted her birth date. She had been born twenty-six years before, the daughter of Henry and Mary Esh. Liz delved a generation earlier. She could not find Mary's birth or parents, but Henry had been born in the 1960s, the son of Ezekiel and Eunice Glick Esh.

So Miriam had been right. Lydia had Glicks in her background.

But proved nothing yet as far as Mr. Whittington was concerned. And during the 1940s, when Henry's parents would have been born, the Glicks, Eshes, and probably many other Amish families preferred to record children's births only among their own congregations. In earlier searches for questions regarding Amish families, Liz had checked online, as some groups had allowed the posting of such historical data. However, the local Amish did not. Nor would they release that information to outsiders if asked, she was sure.

So now Liz turned to property records, as Amish farmers in the past were more likely to submit land transactions for public record than births or marriages. Miriam was right. Dozens of Glicks had recorded the sale and purchase of land through the years. How Liz's fingers itched for a "search" button!

Instead, she tried focusing on Priscilla herself.

Hmm. Priscilla Hertzler had been born in 1920. So if she had come to Indiana as a small child, her adopted father, Solomon Hertzler, had probably bought land sometime during the early 1920s. But after searching the entire decade, Liz had to admit defeat. Not a single Hertzler appeared in the property ownership book. If Priscilla's adoptive father had bought land, he did not record the purchase on public record. Perhaps he did so for the same reasons other Amish did—distrust of outside authorities.

Or maybe Solomon wanted to ensure that Mr. Whittington's father, James, did not find his daughter, Priscilla. Or Sally, his lost love.

Earlier, Liz had come up short when it came to Henry Esh's parents' birth records. Perhaps she would have more luck in tracing the family line through property ownership. She scanned Esh and Glick sales and purchases throughout the 1940s until she thought she would go crazy. Row after row of names and figures nearly lulled her to sleep.

Until one purchase caught her eye. Four acres of land near Pleasant Creek's north side had been purchased by Abel and Priscilla Glick in June 1947.

Priscilla. Liz's pulse rocketed. *Mr. Whittington's Priscilla?*

"May I help you with something?" The secretary bent over Liz's shoulder. A little too friendly. She leaned so low that Liz couldn't move. Was the clerk staring at her notes?

Liz covered them. "Yes, may I have the marriage records from, say, 1930 through 1950?"

If Priscilla had been born in 1920, she probably had married sometime between 1936 and the early 1940s.

The clerk brought the big black book, lingering until Liz assured the woman she did not need more help.

Now far from sleepy, Liz's eyes wanted to run down the columns at the speed of her heartbeat. If only Abel and Priscilla had recorded their marriage here!

They had not.

Liz broadened her search to include possible marriage years from

1934 to 1947, when Priscilla's age would have ranged between fourteen and twenty-seven. She double-checked the pages, a small throb in her forehead swelling into a full-scale headache.

Liz found no record of their marriage, the entry that would have included Priscilla's maiden name, confirming or denying her relationship to Lydia and Mr. Whittington.

Now what? Liz wilted on her hard chair.

She'd hoped today's search might firm up this nebulous quest for Mr. Whittington's relatives, give him a factual basis for talking to Lydia about their common bloodline.

Instead, Liz had hit a documentation wall, with no final answer.

Miriam had no answers either, and little prospect of learning any.

Perhaps that irate stranger knew if Mr. Whittington and Lydia were connected.

Did anyone else?

12

"Isn't this tea set perfectly lovely?" Maxine radiated goodwill that Liz attributed to the fine set as well as to Sadie's absence from coffee hour. The mercurial woman held a small teacup of espresso, her plump pinkie poised just so.

Liz, serving Naomi's miniature éclairs of every color and flavor, hoped her difficult guest would keep her smile intact throughout the next hour.

Surely there was every reason to think she might. Mr. Whittington, dressed for the occasion in long evening tails and an orange-striped golf shirt, was playing host with impeccable charm. He'd supplied English teas in addition to the espresso—black currant, Darjeeling, and a special blend in honor of the queen's ninetieth birthday. But Naomi's treats alone—the éclairs, scones filled with fruit and topped with whipped cream, as well as rich lemon and blackberry jam cake—made this special English tea and coffee hour a memorable event.

Kyle Stinson seemed to think so. He paid little attention to the tea set Megan, his wife, admired. But he dove into the snacks with such unbridled enthusiasm that the rest of the group, including the Brumpetts, Mary Ann, Caitlyn, and Opal, couldn't help sharing his joy in the excellent food.

Megan merely shook her head at him. Her tiny fingers seemed made to hold Sherry's teacups.

As they feasted and admired the delicate china, Mr. Whittington regaled them with stories of his sojourns in England: the occasions he'd seen the queen and her family, and hiking through picturesque towns featuring cottages with thatched roofs. Sitting between the Brumpett sisters, Mr. Whittington somehow kept them from tearing him—and each other—in two.

He smiled as he spoke of Sherry, especially his daughter's wanting to bring strangers home to have tea with her and her dolls "so they won't be lonesome, Daddy."

His listeners' tears mirrored his own, as did their chuckles when he told how Sherry had talked him out of grounding her by discussing the matter over the cookies and tea she'd made just for him.

"She always could wind her old dad around her pretty little finger," he admitted.

Liz wondered if Mr. Whittington would bring up anything he'd told her earlier—about his search for his half sister, about the similar tea sets. But he didn't mention those, so Liz didn't either.

Coffee hour stretched an extra hour, by the end of which everyone felt like part of the Whittington family. Even the Brumpetts helped clear up, and Liz rejoiced to sense the change in the atmosphere.

Until, having seen Mr. Whittington take an evening walk toward the lake, Liz spotted Maxine five minutes later, jogging through the inn's backyard toward him.

Liz wanted to tackle the woman!

"Marlene seems to have taken the hint. But how," she said to the other Material Girls as they helped wash dishes, "can Maxine be so completely obtuse? They might be friends if she didn't hunt him like prey."

Before her words died, someone burst through the inn's front door.

Liz hurried into the rotunda. "Is that you, Mr. Whittington?"

"That infernal woman!" Liz's normally amiable guest, his white hair rumpled, now resembled an enraged cockatoo. "I barely escaped with my life!"

"I am so sorry—"

He started to dash for the stairs, only to encounter a smiling Maxine blocking the way. "Dear Mr. Whittington," she cooed, "you misunderstood me—"

"Oh, no." He backed away, gritting his teeth. "I understand you perfectly. It is you who cannot comprehend common courtesy. Therefore, I shall abandon it as a language you do not speak." Glaring, he yelled, "Leave me *alone*!"

Liz blinked.

Maxine blinked. But her smile returned, toothier than ever. "My, you do play hard to get. But I play hard as well."

"No, madam." Now he shoved his red face into hers. "I am not interested in you. I shall *never* be interested in you. I am not playing hard to get. And if you continue to harass me, I shall have a restraining order put on you. Do. I. Make. Myself. Clear?"

Apparently, he made himself clear to the Stinsons, who peered over the top of the stairway, eyes wide.

Liz realized she was holding a spatula covered with gooey blackberry jam. Not her weapon of choice, but she'd use it if necessary. The other Material Girls, her backup, filled the rotunda door.

Maxine stared down her nose, eyes glittering like balls of ice. "I'm all about forgiving and forgetting, so I overlooked your rudeness the other day. But twice? Never!"

She wobbled up the stairs, the futile tap-tap of her stilettos echoing thinly through the rotunda.

The Stinsons fled before she reached the top.

The Material Girls disappeared.

Liz and Mr. Whittington stared.

His face broke into the only truly wicked smile she'd seen him wear. He whispered, "I do hope she means every word."

Liz loved her inn and rarely craved time away from it.

After yesterday's excitement, though, Sadie's campout sounded like the R & R opportunity of the year.

The Brumpetts had not stormed out of the inn, as Liz had secretly hoped. But she hated to dump the situation on Miriam.

"Thank goodness Mr. Whittington and the twins have ignored each other—so far." Liz handed a last-minute instruction sheet to Miriam. "You're a brave woman to substitute for me right now."

Her cousin permitted herself a small eye roll. "I have six children. I believe I can manage."

Probably better than I can. Liz ached for time away from conflicts, from the nagging search for Mr. Whittington's relatives. The creepy phone calls. And the culprits behind the vandalisms.

Perhaps her glowering guests needed a hostess change too.

The drive to the state park proved relaxing. The cool luxury of her Acura mollified Liz's fatigue, and soft jazz soothed her angst. Best of all, sweet solitude breathed life into her.

But why had she agreed to spend a night in the wild, armed only with sleeping bag, backpack, and deep-woods bug spray? And she was facing more than the traditional kind of wild. A birthday overnight with Sadie and the other Material Girls? The park ranger might toss them out in the wee hours.

Approaching the state park's gate, Liz almost kept going. A billboard advertised an air-conditioned hotel a mile ahead.

Smart innkeeper, she mused. *Perfect location for a sign to capture camping cowards.*

Liz turned toward the gate.

After parking at the campground's entrance, she consulted a map.

Painted numbers had faded from some campsite signs. Would she have to hike every loop before finding the birthday bash?

Liz need not have worried.

Not only did the pink camo camper stand out, but Sadie had strung blinking pink, purple, and blue lights throughout the campsite.

Sadie waved frantically and, putting her fingers to her mouth, greeted Liz with an excruciating whistle that evoked canine howls nearby.

As Liz approached the campsite, she realized that one canine hadn't been disturbed by Sadie's greeting. Beans lay on his rug directly in front of the camper's door, snoring.

"Girl, I am so glad you came." Sadie's fervent hug chased away Liz's doubts.

"Happy birthday, Sadie."

Echoes from Mary Ann, Naomi, and Caitlyn brought a huge smile to Sadie's face and another to Liz's. How could she have considered bypassing this special time with friends?

Quickly, they headed for the beach, clinging to Sadie's Jeep as it roared up and down hills.

How wonderful, Liz mused, *to have friends so dear that neither they nor I care about how we look in bathing suits.*

They arrived when most swimmers and water-skiers were leaving, probably for supper. The golden sun still kissed the shimmering lake. Fresh water washed away their cares. They tossed Frisbees, beach balls, and each other. Liz, with Sadie on her shoulders, hadn't played chicken fight since middle school, but she and Sadie dunked Caitlyn and Naomi three times out of five, according to Mary Ann, who assumed the role of referee. At the end, the four contestants ganged up to dunk the referee.

Caitlyn proclaimed, "Nobody at this campout is allowed perfect hair—not even Mary Ann."

Mary Ann accepted this with her usual grace.

Starved after swimming, they picked up Chinese takeout from a restaurant Sadie tagged as her favorite. Liz had never pictured munching sweet-and-sour chicken and egg rolls at a picnic table, but tonight, they seemed the perfect outdoor fare. *Mmm, delicious.*

Opal would have enjoyed the Chinese feast. Liz missed her. Because of the tensions between her and Sadie, no one had mentioned their sixth member, but Liz was sure the other Material Girls also wished Opal had joined them.

After supper, Naomi, a former Girl Scout, built a fire, arranging the wood just so.

Caitlyn handed out hot dog sticks and marshmallows. "I made Sadie's s'mores cake, but you all need to roast marshmallows for the topping."

They were readying their marshmallows when a voice said, "Think you can roast 'em without burning them all to a crisp?"

Opal.

She wore an odd sideways smile. She also wore jeans—the first time Liz had seen her in them.

"We can cook 'em as well as you can." Sadie, her eyes wet, threw her arms around her friend.

"No, you can't," Opal retorted, while the others cheered and joined in a group hug.

She was right, of course. With Opal's expert roasting technique, her marshmallows turned golden brown.

Liz blackened several and actually set one on fire, which she willingly shared with Beans, whose sticky muzzle then had to be washed.

Caitlyn had opened a can of hot fudge and set it on the grill, stirring it with a long fork. When the others had browned twenty marshmallows, she poured the fudge over a big chocolate cake, then plopped the marshmallows on top.

"Where are the graham crackers? Not that I'm complaining,"

Naomi added as Caitlyn swirled the marshmallows into the fudge.

"I crumbled them into marshmallow cream between layers."

"Well, where are the candles? Isn't anybody going to sing, 'Happy Birthday'?" Sadie demanded.

Caitlyn lit enough candles to set the forest ablaze while everyone sang and Mary Ann took pictures. Then they demolished the s'mores cake, the richest and stickiest Liz had ever eaten.

And Opal didn't once complain about her hair.

Liz gathered the gifts before Sadie could demand those as well. Taking a cue from Mr. Whittington, she'd found a tractor made of stained glass for Sadie.

"It'll go in my front kitchen window," said the birthday girl.

Naomi had bought her a colorful hand-knitted scarf for fall. Mary Ann had transferred a picture of Sadie's grandchildren to a pillow cover she'd quilted. Caitlyn had embroidered Sadie's initials on a denim tote for her sewing supplies.

"And this is from Opal." Sadie opened the last package, a small, beautifully wrapped box.

Her eyes widened. Her jaw dropped.

Sadie took a small purple ribbon from the box. "Is this—is it—"

"Yes." Opal nodded, her lip quivering. "The grand champion ribbon for beginner sewing at the 1960 county fair."

Everyone stared.

Liz inhaled. *You two have been fighting about that apron-sewing competition for the past fifty-plus years.*

Sadie walked slowly to Opal, took her hand, and squeezed it. "Thanks," she said quietly.

After a few subdued minutes, the usual chatter returned, with oohing and ahhing over Sadie's gifts. As the fire burned down and glittering crystal stars began to crowd the black-velvet sky, Caitlyn, the best singer, led every camp song she knew. Sadie told her lamest jokes and scariest ghost stories.

Liz enjoyed the evening so much she didn't mind the muggy heat or the few mosquitoes that seemed to love repellent. *If only I could stay here forever.*

She hadn't in a million years expected that thought to surface.

It didn't linger though, when they went to bed after midnight. Everyone drew straws. Mary Ann and Caitlyn, with the longest straws, chose the queen-sized bed on one end. Sadie and Opal chose the other. Liz and Naomi faced sleeping on the table.

Liz tried to cheer herself. *We do have a mattress.* And this arrangement worked much better than sleeping on the ground, where giant snakes could slither into her sleeping bag. When she said as much to Naomi, her friend replied, "Thanks for the perspective adjustment. I think."

The camper's screens would have provided decent airflow had air been flowing. But the humidity increased with every hour, and even when Liz lay on top of her sleeping bag, the night weighed on her like wet wool.

Even Beans slept poorly, groaning, rolling, and giving disconsolate sighs. Sadie had insisted he would catch cold if left outside. When Beans did sleep, Liz could have sworn his snores raised the camper's canvas top.

Stay here forever? I don't think so.

But only one night? She could do this.

A low growl filled the air. It didn't sound like Beans.

Thunder. Liz raised her head as shards of lightning sliced the sky.

"Maybe the rain will drown me and put me out of my misery," Naomi mumbled.

"This camper's guaranteed one hundred percent waterproof." Sadie had awakened too.

She was right. The wind-driven monsoon gently rocked the camper, and they had to zip the plastic windows shut. The Material Girls slowly boiled.

"Now I know what a poached egg feels like." Even Mary Ann groused a little.

"Or a lobster," Caitlyn added.

Opal said nothing.

No "I told you so"? *You are some kind of woman, Opal Ringenberg.*

Eventually the rain lessened to a gentle patter, and they unzipped the windows at the top.

"Sweet oxygen." Liz, kneeling on their "bed," inhaled deeply.

"I'd forgotten what it tasted like." Naomi followed suit.

The cooler air did make the camper bearable, and the thunder's low rumbles joined the rain's pitter-patter to play a pleasant lullaby. Liz finally dozed off.

Only to be awakened by a small but sharp *crack* outside the camper.

The sound woke Beans too. He barked as if he wanted to tear someone apart.

"What's the matter, boy?" Her skin prickling, Liz tried to soothe the bulldog.

Instead, Beans scratched frantically at the linoleum, barking and growling as if possessed.

"Shut *up*, Beans," Caitlyn's foggy voice groaned from one bed.

"Don't yell at him!" Sadie ordered. "Something's upsetting him terribly. Can't you calm him, Liz?"

With difficulty, Liz controlled her voice. "He doesn't *want* to calm down. I'm guessing some animal is out there. Probably under the camper, the way he's scratching the floor."

She shivered. Had Bingo Guy followed her here? The stranger from the courthouse? Or even Mr. Whittington?

Sadie muttered, "Guess I'll have to take care of Beans myself."

As Liz contemplated the penalty for aggravated assault in Indiana, Sadie slid off the bed.

The floor of the camper on that side tilted crazily.

So did the bed.

With a screeching Opal in it.

Liz crawled along what had been the floor. "Don't follow me," she shouted to the others. "The floor's collapsed. It won't hold our weight."

Beans added howls to his angry repertoire.

"Sadie, Opal, are you all right?" Mary Ann shouted.

"I'm okay," Sadie called.

"I'm just jim-dandy."

Liz had to smother a laugh. Sarcasm oozed from Opal's every syllable.

Sadie yelled again, "Just take care of Beans, will you?"

Ignoring the rain, Caitlyn grabbed a flashlight and snapped on the bulldog's leash. Opening the door, she gasped.

A huge, hooded figure blocked the doorway.

Beans went berserk.

"I'm Eric Andrews, the park ranger," the man roared above the noise. "Call off your dog!"

Liz searched the cabinets frantically for a treat while Sadie slowly crawled out of the jumbled mass of sleeping bags, pillows, and canvas, Opal following her.

"Hush!"

Liz jumped. Had Sadie ever spoken like that to Beans?

Apparently not, for it startled him into silence.

"Thank you." The ranger glanced from person to person. "Are you all okay?"

We're just jim-dandy.

"I think so," Sadie said. "But I'm wondering if the supports on this side of the camper somehow gave way. Could you help me check it out?"

Ranger Andrews—who was quite good-looking—didn't appear enthusiastic about the prospect. But he and Sadie, joined by Caitlyn, trudged into the rain with flashlights. Liz, Naomi, and Opal moved to the other end of the camper with Mary Ann while the others banged and yanked. Slowly, the floor straightened and returned to its rightful position.

Beans, however, had begun his crazy barking again. While the others stuffed him with treats, Liz grabbed a flashlight and rain poncho. She shone its beam all around the camper. Stooping, she saw movement behind the front wheels. She banged on the floor to scare away whatever it was before thinking, *What if it's a skunk?*

Fortunately, a mother raccoon and three babies skittered out from under the camper and ran into the woods.

Whew. Thank goodness they hadn't taken Beans outside earlier. Raccoons looked cute, but they could be ferocious.

"Ladies," the ranger called through the camper walls, "please do not leave this site. We appear to be dealing with a prowler."

Her muscles froze. When they thawed a few seconds later, Liz slipped outside to the rear of the camper, where flashlights were focused on large, muddy footprints.

"I *knew* I installed those supports right when I set up." Sadie pointed to the thick metal bars she and the others had restored to their correct position. "Somebody came after the rain started and yanked them loose."

Maybe Liz's nighttime paranoia wasn't so paranoid after all. "I did hear something outside just before the camper's collapse. Beans probably did too—I thought he was only barking at raccoons."

"I saw someone running away from this site into the woods," the ranger said grimly. "Too dark and rainy to see whom. Thought I'd better check on you ladies rather than chase him."

Eric called the sheriff, who promptly appeared to question everyone. Since eight people in the camper were a tight fit, they took turns sitting in Sadie's Jeep. By the time the sheriff had finished his interviews, the rain had stopped, and a rooster at a nearby farm let loose his cheery cock-a-doodle-doo.

The Materials Girls were weaving on their feet.

We're too tired to break camp. Leaving it all behind and trying to drive home would be downright dangerous.

Eric grasped the situation. "You ladies need sleep. Feel free to go back to bed. I'll remain outside your camper for a couple of hours." He flashed a drop-dead-gorgeous smile at Caitlyn. "And if you need anything, anything at all, just let me know."

They gratefully rearranged the sleeping bags and the contents of two cabinets that had spilled out with the mini-earthquake.

The night's events had taken their toll on Beans. He flopped down where he stood, snoring before he hit the floor.

"Well," Sadie said, "it's certainly been a birthday I won't forget."

I don't think any of us will. No matter how hard we try.

"I think maybe we'd better just do the one night after all, even though I'd planned for two," she added regretfully.

"Sadie, we don't have to cut your celebration short just because of some creep," Caitlyn protested, but it was halfhearted.

"No, I don't mind. I just bought this camper and I'm not going to risk it getting permanently damaged," Sadie replied. Then her face brightened. "Next time, things will go better."

Next time? The air shook with silent exclamation points.

But without a word, they followed Beans's astute example.

Liz endeavored to shrink her frame so she wouldn't crowd Naomi.

Maybe that's what getaways were for.

They made you want to go back home.

13

Perspiring with the late morning heat, Liz pushed the inn's front door open, anticipating the usual rush of cool, refreshing air.

If anything, she sweated more.

"Oh, no. Not air-conditioning problems again," she groaned. On a Saturday yet.

"I'm afraid so." Miriam appeared with a tall glass of ice water, which Liz downed. "When I awoke, I opened all the windows, but I have begun shutting them again, as the thermometer says it is already ninety degrees outside."

"How long will it take me to find a repairman this time?" Liz wondered aloud. She'd caught the first one right before he left for a two-week vacation.

At least the feud between Mr. Whittington and Maxine hadn't heated up more.

"I think they're trying to avoid each other," Miriam reported. "The Brumpett women went out for breakfast this morning, as did Mr. Whittington." Her eyes twinkled. "I hope they all did not go to Mama's."

Liz slapped her forehead. "Did they tell you before you prepared a big breakfast?"

"You may have extra baked goods for tomorrow morning, which is a good thing, after having been gone." Miriam touched Liz's shoulder, her indigo eyes full of sympathy. "You called me a brave woman. I think you are brave for returning."

Yay, me.

"Speaking of returning," Miriam continued, "last evening, a Mr.

Tony Lanham appeared and asked for a room for the night. He said he'd stayed here before, and I gave him the Sunrise Room."

"Yes, he stayed here last week." Odd that Tony hadn't mentioned he would return. "Is he still here?"

"No, he left immediately after breakfast."

Whatever Tony's reason, a returning guest was positive. Liz thanked Miriam profusely as they said good-bye, then began another round of phone calls to repairmen.

The Stinsons, coming from the dining room, told Liz they hadn't noticed the lack of air-conditioning until they awoke. They had particularly enjoyed breakfast.

"Your cousin's quiet, but man, she can cook!" Kyle bestowed his highest praise.

Maybe the couple brushed off the air-conditioning problems because they were leaving this morning. Whatever the reason, Liz appreciated their exuberance and easygoing attitudes despite the conflicts between the other guests.

When she tried to apologize, Kyle grinned. "Actually, it was fun watching those old people duke it out."

Liz waved as the Stinsons went on their merry, carefree way. Maybe someday she'd see this senior soap opera as funny too.

Jackson called, annoyingly cheerful. "Did you stay dry during the thunderstorm last night?"

"Dry? Um, yes." He'd only called to check on her this morning, but too bad. He'd hear the rest.

After her account of the night's events, he whistled. "Wow. Sounds like you need a vacation from your vacation."

"Don't tempt me."

"How about a mini-vacation—seeing a movie with me in Fort Wayne tonight?"

Tony and the Stinsons had left, but the Brumpetts wouldn't until tomorrow. Besides, did she want these daily check-in calls to turn into something bigger? "I have a ton to do. May I take a rain check?"

"Sure. Anytime." His voice lost its levity. "Be sure to tell Houghton about your prowler."

"I will." Overwhelmed by another air-conditioning disaster, she'd forgotten to contact the chief.

"I'll call you later." Jackson hung up faster than Liz had anticipated.

She'd wanted some space, hadn't she? Yet disappointment clouded her morning further.

Liz went to the dining room to clear up, only to find Kyle had devoured all the extra baked goods. *How . . . obliging of him.*

Thankfully, Miriam had cleaned up most of the kitchen mess. Liz alternated housework, making phone calls, and listening to the Brumpetts complain about the heat. She offered to find them a hotel where they could stay the last night. Marlene agreed, but no, no, no, Maxine loved the Rose of Sharon Room too much to leave it early.

Liz suspected that an opportunity to gripe trumped all other hotel amenities. Was Maxine also planning one more scheme to infuriate Mr. Whittington? In Maxine's eyes, enduring the sticky heat might prove worth it.

However, Mr. Whittington was wisely making himself scarce.

The lone bright spot in the too-bright, sweltering afternoon was that a repairman offered to come Monday morning.

Liz made smoothies again for coffee hour, which she enjoyed, but did not appease the Brumpetts. Again, Mr. Whittington was nowhere to be seen. Thank goodness.

After surviving coffee hour, Liz took a swim, letting Jaynes Lake's peaceful scenery and cool, refreshing water wash away the flush in her fevered face, the furrows in her forehead.

She recommended a swim to the Brumpetts, only to be met with horrified gasps of "*Germs!*" and predictions of Liz's contracting dire diseases.

Those two could reverse a good thing in record time. When the phone rang, she nearly answered with, "Mr. Repairman, you'd better not be canceling!" Instead she managed to say, "Olde Mansion Inn, Liz speaking."

Hoarse breathing.

Not again.

A different phone number from the others had flashed on the screen.

Smash!

A blow sounded on the other end of the line, as if someone were demolishing china. A sickening cascade of fragments hit a floor.

Then she heard only the dial tone.

Shaking, Liz wanted to throw the phone to the floor and smash it too.

Instead, she called Chief Houghton.

The chief didn't say it, but Liz heard it in his tone: *You just won't back off, will you?*

She gritted her teeth. "For the record, I've done very little related to the burglaries since that stupid package arrived. I did give a tea party. Well, actually, one of my guests hosted one."

"A what?"

"A tea party. With a very special tea set." She told Houghton about Mr. Whittington's quest and the possibility of Lydia being his half sister's descendant. "Given the smashed teacup package and now this horrible phone call, don't you think Mr. Whittington's mission might be linked to my harassment? And maybe the burglaries?"

"Sure would seem so. He could have weird relatives who hate the Amish."

"But he has no relatives," Liz protested. "His wife and only daughter are dead, and he was an only child, other than his half sister." Liz bit her lip. "Like me, he came to Pleasant Creek searching for family. That's why I wanted to help him."

"Sounds like I need to talk to Mr. Whittington." Houghton's tone hardened.

"Probably a good idea," Liz agreed, "though I've seen no evidence he's done anything wrong."

A sigh on the other end. "I just want to catch the creeps who are causing all the trouble, Liz. I need to explore everything."

"I know." Liz told the chief that Mr. Whittington had just paid for another week's stay, so he'd be around. "But I doubt he'll return to the inn before late this evening. He's been ducking an aggressive lady guest who isn't leaving until tomorrow."

Houghton chuckled. "Sounds like he—and you—have had fun this week."

"Have I ever."

He laughed outright when she summarized their confrontation and the campout. But his mirth died when she mentioned the prowler.

"I'll call that sheriff and the park ranger," the chief said, "and no more campouts for you until we catch these perps."

She could live with that. Liz added, "I did spend a couple of hours searching records at the courthouse for Mr. Whittington."

She also told him about the antagonistic researcher she'd encountered.

"Hmm. Could have been someone on the same track as you," Houghton surmised, "or it could have been some genealogy nut who thinks she owns the courthouse."

He took her description of the girl. "We'll keep an eye out for her. Don't you go looking, okay? Just stay cool and calm."

"I'd love to," Liz said, "if I could." She related her air-conditioning struggles.

Houghton sympathized. "Boy, you didn't need that."

"You know," Liz said, choosing her words carefully. "I've tried my best to stay out of trouble, Chief. And all along, I've told you everything." She paused. "Do you think you could trust me with a little of what's happening on your end?"

He was quiet for so long she didn't think he'd answer. Finally, he said, "I guess I could tell you I got a lead on who did that burglary at the Wickeys.'"

She gripped the phone. "Who?"

"Found out Gideon Sommer had wanted to marry that little Kirchhofer girl, but she married Laban Wickey instead, and he's been mad ever since. I just talked to an Amish witness who saw Gideon and a couple of other Rumschpringe guys along the road near the Wickey farm that night."

A witness. "Do you think that will shake them?"

"I hope so. I hope one of 'em will cave and tell me the truth. With an eyewitness from their congregation putting them near the scene, their families and the bishop will get involved. If I can't encourage a confession, I imagine the bishop can."

"That fits the damage I saw at the Wickeys'. Vindictiveness, with no other apparent purpose. But how would that be linked to the smashed china cup and the phone calls? And what does that have to do with the Kings?" Liz puzzled. "I only met Gideon once. Would he see me as a threat? And if he wanted to harass someone, would he use a teacup?"

"No," Houghton snorted. "But maybe something else will come to light as I talk with those Amish boys."

Since he'd told her about one lead, maybe he'd open up about another. Liz coaxed, "Did you ask Harvey who bought those extra place settings of my dishes?"

The chief exhaled. "Yeah, but he wasn't much help. Said he sold them over the weekend, when his help was sick and his shop was full of tourists. He couldn't even remember whether it was a man or woman. Whoever bought them must have used cash, because nothing turned up in his receipts."

Liz didn't know much more than she had before phoning Houghton, but at least the chief was including her in the loop again.

"Remember, I want you to stay clear of all this." His no-nonsense voice interrupted her thoughts. "You haven't seen that pigeon-toed guy again, have you?"

"No." Though she wouldn't be at all surprised if Bingo Guy and Phone Guy were one and the same. "If I do, I'll let you know."

"Yeah, don't try to sell him bingo tickets again, okay?"

She wanted to point out that Mary Ann had done that, but the chief chuckled and hung up.

Pleasant Creek hadn't received rain since the storm, and the evening hadn't cooled much. Still, Liz considered doing yardwork to avoid her guests. Since Kiera had left for college, the grounds had suffered. Prying weeds out of dusty, cement-hard flower beds didn't sound like a fun way to spend a Saturday night, but then, life wasn't always fun. Besides, it was better than facing the stiff tension between her guests.

She'd pulled exactly three weeds when her phone rang. She jumped, in spite of herself. But Phone Man had only called her landline. He didn't know her cell number. Did he?

It was Jackson.

"Checking in early for two reasons. One, the chief says you received a really nasty phone call from that jerk. Second, how do you feel about maybe going to a movie now?"

That sounded fun. With no sweat. "Which movie?"

"You can pick when we get there. Or we can see them all."

She laughed. "If their air-conditioning works, I'm in."

"Pick you up in a half hour?"

"Sure. Thanks." She hung up and gathered her gardening tools. "Sorry, zinnias, but I'm out of here."

Though she doubted makeup would survive ten minutes of this humidity, Liz applied some and changed into a sundress.

She'd braved the wilds last night. Tonight, she'd savor the joys of civilization—and being with Jackson.

He really was a fun guy. He kept her smiling and helped her forget the stuff that had made her crazy lately. The movie they picked was just right—suspenseful, but not terrifying; funny, but not silly; romantic, but not sugary.

By the time they returned to the inn, Liz had lost twenty years. Maybe they could prolong the magic?

But the minute she opened the front door, Mr. Whittington accosted them, wringing his hands. "Thank God you're here."

His face had turned ashen, and he swayed as if about to lose his balance. Jackson grabbed his arm and steadied him. Liz clasped his hand. "Mr. Whittington, let me take you to the emergency room."

He buried his face in his hands. "No, no, I must find it."

"Find what?" Liz rubbed his shoulder. "Can we help you find it?"

"Sherry's tea set." His look of despair made him look, for the first time, like a frightened old man. "It's gone."

14

"What?" Liz cried. She threw an arm around Mr. Whittington's shaking shoulders while Jackson ran to grab her desk chair. "When did it go missing?"

"Sometime today while I was gone." He sank onto the chair, limp as a rag doll.

She wanted to say, "Never mind about the tea set. Let's take care of you." But that would only agitate him further. Jackson stayed with him while Liz brought a glass of water.

She gently rubbed his shoulder. A little color came into the old man's face, but he still drooped as if he'd never straighten again. "I locked the door before I left early this morning. It was locked when I returned." He wrung his hands again. "Someone must have climbed that big maple outside and slid the screen open, then closed it when he left."

Liz and Jackson exchanged glances. Pleasant Creek citizens looked out for each other. How could an intruder have entered and escaped, carrying that big box of fragile china, without someone noticing? Now that she thought of it, how would someone have climbed down the maple carrying the box at all?

"I guess it's possible." She thought out loud before she realized it. "The maple's foliage blocks that window completely from a street view, with large shrubs between the maple's trunk and the sidewalk. And with the air-conditioning broken—"

"Yes, I'd left my window open so my room wouldn't be sweltering when I returned."

Now she wanted to hide her face. Mr. Whittington had suffered terrible, maybe irreparable loss because of her stupid air-conditioning?

"I'll call Chief Houghton." Jackson pulled out his phone.

"The police? No, no!" the man exclaimed, eyes wide and glassy.

"It's all right, Mr. Whittington," Liz soothed, as if he were a child. "The chief is my good friend, an officer who cares. He'll find your tea set."

Mr. Whittington made no answer. He hunched, fingers fiddling with the cuffs of his silky 1970s disco shirt.

Houghton and two officers arrived promptly. The chief wiped his forehead. "Air-conditioning still on the fritz?"

Gritting her teeth, Liz nodded.

He patted her shoulder, then sent Officers Dixon and Hughes upstairs to collect fingerprints and other evidence while he talked to Cyrus.

The distraught man had calmed somewhat, though little trace of the dapper octogenarian showed. They adjourned to the sitting room for more privacy.

At first, Mr. Whittington would say nothing.

If he wanted Sherry's tea set back, why was he stonewalling the police? Liz's lawyer sense nagged her. What was he hiding?

Eventually, though, with the chief's laid-back interview style, Cyrus cooperated. Though he mumbled his answers, the information he provided made sense. Liz was also encouraged that he'd recalled the day in correct chronological order. Perhaps the trauma of the theft had only temporarily scrambled his faculties.

Suddenly she realized she'd thought of him by his first name. As she looked at him again, she realized how dear he had become to her. Her heart ached as she looked at him now, so small and vulnerable, without any trace of his usual panache.

"Is anything else missing or damaged?" Houghton asked. "Any money stolen?"

Why hadn't she thought to ask that? Liz clicked her tongue. With all the burglaries afoot, that should have been her first query—

Her lungs emptied. Had anything else been stolen from the other guests? From her inn?

"I—I hadn't really noticed," Cyrus mumbled. "My glass elephant, I think. And some jars. Perhaps more." He slumped again.

"Do you have any idea who might have done this?" Houghton asked.

Cyrus's normally bright-blue eyes had turned slate-gray. "I can't imagine who would steal Sherry's tea set."

"The police—again?" Maxine yelled from the doorway.

Liz jumped. She *knew* she'd closed the sitting room door.

But the woman had poked her head inside. How long had she been listening?

"Dear, oh dear," Marlene's distressed voice echoed throughout the rotunda.

"What kind of inn is this?" Maxine shrilled. "And what has that—that rascal been up to?" She pointed to Mr. Whittington.

"Stop right there, ma'am." Houghton placed his stocky frame between her and the sofa where Cyrus had sat up, eyes glinting. The chief continued, "There's been a burglary, of which this gentleman is a victim. You are a guest here, correct?"

His steely, professional tone worked wonders.

"Er—yes." She bobbed her head uncertainly.

"Please go immediately to your room and check if anything's missing. Make a list, and remain there until I come to speak with you."

Maxine closed the door, and Liz heard the tap-tap of her stilettos up the stairs.

Whoa. Liz considered asking Houghton to stay until Maxine left.

They waited a few minutes, then Liz scouted the second floor to make sure the two had followed his direction. She motioned to the men below. Jackson helped the old man up the stairs, Houghton accompanying them.

When they entered the Somewhere in Time Room, Officer Dixon reported, "Nothing smashed or torn up, like at the other burglaries."

If only the rest of the inn had been spared. Liz's hands tightened into fists.

Houghton sent Dixon back to the station with fingerprints they'd collected. The chief ordered Officer Hughes to search the rest of the inn for any other signs of a break-in. Liz handed him her ring of labeled keys.

Mr. Whittington glanced at his glass collection, then removed a Perry Como album from its rack. He pulled an old leather wallet from its lumpy hiding place inside the cover and examined it. "They didn't take my money."

Houghton, looking over Cyrus's shoulder, blinked. Having received all her payments from Mr. Whittington in cash, Liz didn't have to imagine the hundred-dollar bills the wallet contained.

The chief advised, "Given this break-in, I'd keep that in Liz's safe, if I were you, sir."

Cyrus nodded and handed it to her, then shuffled over to his glass collection. "Yes. My elephant has disappeared, as have my two Ball jars." Face puckering, he scanned the groupings for several minutes, touching them as if they were his children. His compressed mouth relaxed. "All the others seem to be here."

Still clearly distraught, he refused the tea Liz offered and asked to go to bed.

"Certainly. You've had a rough evening," the chief said. "We will do everything we can to find your tea set, Mr. Whittington."

He nodded as if hearing a recording.

Liz patted him on the shoulder. "Let me know if you need anything at all."

After they left the Somewhere in Time Room, Houghton said, "Only you can really tell if something's missing from your inn. Can you do a search whilst I talk with those . . . ladies?"

Something in his tone said he'd rather interview hardened criminals.

"All right." Liz dreaded knowing, yet longed to start. "Do you think I should call Mary Ann to have her check Sew Welcome?"

"She'd want to know. Call her."

He was right. Mary Ann would want to be on top of everything. Liz pulled out her phone.

The time read eleven thirty. After last night's camping fiasco, how could she awaken her friend with such lousy news? But she did.

"No. Don't want any," her friend slurred sleepily.

"Mary Ann, I'm not a telemarketer. Somebody stole stuff from Mr. Whittington's room today."

"What?" In a second, Mary Ann became Mary Ann. "Is he all right?"

"He's shaken, but I think he'll be okay."

"What did the creep take this time?"

Liz hated to even say it. "Sherry's tea set."

She heard a sharp intake of breath. "That's unspeakable."

"Yes. Mr. Whittington's really upset." Liz sighed. "I hated to bother you, but the chief said you should know."

"I'll be right there."

Since she was already upstairs, Liz hurried to check the unoccupied guest rooms, Jackson striding beside her.

"I don't know this place like you do, but maybe I can move heavy furniture or whatever," he offered.

"You don't have to do this." Liz unlocked the Heritage Room. "Not exactly a fun ending to the evening."

"I'm never bored around you," he joked.

She couldn't help smiling. "Well, that's true." By simple associa-tion, he'd seemed to inherit almost every harrowing experience she'd encountered in Pleasant Creek.

And tonight, as always, his presence eased her tensions.

Liz hadn't expected anything missing there or on the third floor. After all, how many trees could the guy climb? And she was right.

On returning to the main floor, Houghton's officer told her nothing had been jimmied. "Your desk appears undisturbed as far as I can see, ma'am. But you may have electronics, a petty cash stash, or something else I don't know about, so please take a close look."

Would her inn escape relatively unscathed when other burglary victims had suffered such terrible damage? Liz checked, Jackson providing a second "objective" view, as he called it.

The rotunda desk area looked exactly as she had left it.

Liz was unlocking the door to her quarters when Sadie burst through the front door, Mary Ann close behind.

"Is Cyrus all right?" Sadie's taut words matched her face.

"I think he'll be fine after a good night's sleep," Liz assured her.

"Is Beans okay?" Sadie's voice broke. She dropped beside the comatose bulldog, who barely flicked an ear.

Liz said, "If he were any more relaxed, he wouldn't have a heartbeat." *I should have sold him to Tony.*

Tony.

Tony who had abruptly showed up yesterday and quickly left this morning. Was he the nice, everyday guy he appeared to be? Or had he taken Mr. Whittington's tea set with him?

"This is getting ridiculous." Mary Ann's dark eyes snapped. "Another burglary? What next?"

"I think I'll start staying the night here," Sadie declared. "With my shotgun."

Oh, that will make everything better. Liz, still stunned at her newest musings, exchanged worried glances with Jackson.

He said, "So far, the thief stole only from Mr. Whittington's room, and the police didn't find anything jimmied. So far it looks like he didn't take anything else."

While Mary Ann and Sadie entered Sew Welcome, Officer Hughes talked briefly with Jackson about some town business. Liz hurried inside her apartment and pushed aside wall panels that hid the built-in wall safe.

Good. No damage to the lock, and its contents—including a large amount for deposit—were intact. She slipped Mr. Whittington's money into the safe, closed it, and slid the panels back into place.

Her laptop lay on the table, where she'd left it. No one had touched the TV or any other electronics. Jackson returned, and they searched the dining room, the library, and the kitchen.

"I haven't a clue as to what would be missing here," he admitted.

"You'd know if you fixed breakfast every morning for a gang." After opening drawers and cabinets, pantry, refrigerator, and freezer, nothing appeared missing, except—

"My stained glass magnet." A blank spot had appeared where she'd placed the magnet the day she'd brought it home from their factory tour. She searched the refrigerator's sides. No magnet.

"Maybe you stuck it in a drawer? Or Sarah or someone else did?" Jackson suggested.

"Maybe Miriam." Though Liz couldn't picture her handling something so foreign.

Surely no one would steal a magnet. Perhaps the Brumpetts, raiding the fridge while she was gone, might have knocked it loose.

The magnet might have fallen under the fridge. She'd pull it out tomorrow and check.

In the sitting room, Liz scrutinized the fireplace mantel. Had she rotated the little white marble bunny off the arrangement and stuck it in the closet with Easter decorations—or was it indeed missing?

This burglary thing is making me crazy. Along with a thousand other things.

As she waited for the chief in the sitting room, her tired mind churned out conjecture like an overworked machine.

Tony had seemed like such a nice, normal guy. Why would he steal an antique tea set?

Did he even know Mr. Whittington possessed a tea set? The set had been featured at coffee hour between his two stays at the inn.

But had Tony known about Mr. Whittington's set before he came to the inn? Had he failed in a first attempt to steal it, returning to succeed in his second try?

Thank goodness, Jackson rejoined her, interrupting the grinding of her mind's gears.

Returning from his interviews with the Brumpetts, even Houghton showed signs of wear and tear.

"You've spent a week with those two in your house?" he muttered, wiping sweat from his forehead.

"She's a saint." Jackson rolled his eyes.

"I may be the only innkeeper who hasn't thrown them out." *Hmm—maybe that's not just a joke.* It certainly explained why, despite the women's endless complaining, they'd stayed.

"Anyway, nothing was missing from their room." Houghton stuffed his handkerchief back into his pocket. "How about you? Any money gone? Valuables?"

She brushed off his question. "Nothing worth mentioning. I seem to have misplaced a couple of little things, certainly not valuable. It could have been much, much worse."

"Certainly could have, especially if it was done by the same guys." She stared. "You think Gideon and company were behind this?"

"Nope. I arrested them a few hours ago. They're out on bail already, but they're looking at jail time for tearing up the Wickeys' barn. They insist they had nothing to do with vandalizing the Kings' house." The chief shook his head. "Haven't made the smartest choices lately, but I can't imagine they'd risk more years in jail over a teapot."

"Who would?" Liz looked from Houghton to Jackson to Hughes. When one mystery break-in appeared solved, another generated even more confusion.

And after two sleep-deprived nights in a row, she wouldn't even mention Tony as a suspect until she could think straight.

"Well, maybe when we check out fingerprints and such, something will make sense." The chief patted her arm with the usual assurances about their patrolling the area before he and Officer Hughes exited out the back door.

"Even he didn't sound convinced," Liz told Jackson as they drained tall glasses of iced tea.

He looked at his watch. "Nothing makes sense at two in the morning. I'd better go if you're going to get any sleep. But if you hear bumps in the night, no matter how dumb, *call me*." Jackson cupped her chin lightly, turning her gaze to meet his. "Okay?"

Liz didn't realize she was holding her breath until his hand dropped. "Okay."

He nodded and took his leave, having successfully added a layer of confusion about something else in Liz's life. Now she would have real trouble falling asleep . . .

15

We *were* planning to return here on our way home from Michigan." Maxine glared at Liz as if she were responsible for the world's problems. "But this place is crazy. Hotter than Hades, burglars on the loose, police in the house. I'm not so sure now."

Liz managed an insincere apology as they returned their keys, but she didn't help with luggage as the Brumpetts marched out the door. After checking carefully to see if she was alone, Liz released a giant sigh of relief. *Yes!*

She hadn't expected Mr. Whittington to appear at breakfast, and he hadn't. After last night's excitement, perhaps he'd like her to bring it to him. She took a cup of black currant tea to his room and tapped on the door.

He swung it open. "Are they gone? Truly gone?"

Forcing herself not to stare at his red-and-black Chinese bathrobe, she nodded with a broad grin.

He clasped his hands. "Thanks be to God!"

Stifling giggles, she handed him the tea.

He took a long sip. "I'm afraid that was a very sincere prayer—one I shall have to repent of at church today. But surely the Almighty Himself sometimes finds those two difficult to tolerate."

She offered to bring him breakfast, but he gloried in his newfound freedom and said he would come to the dining room in a few minutes.

As she warmed bacon-and-egg casserole, Liz mused that she'd have plenty of repenting to do as well. But despite the theft of his tea set, more than a hint of Mr. Whittington's sparkle had returned.

When he appeared, he'd dressed for church, adding a horrific designer tie of mottled purples, greens, and oranges to a spiffy plaid shirt. Not the same plaid as his slippers. She took it as another sign he was feeling better.

Liz hated to bring up last night, but she still didn't understand his resistance to contacting the police. After breakfast, when he was enjoying a second cup of tea, she asked him.

He sighed. "I realize my reaction appeared foolish. Certainly it was, if I want to recover Sherry's tea set. But don't you see that my difficulties in communicating with the Amish community will only increase with my involvement with the police?"

He had a point. Liz patted his hand. "It's all so complicated, isn't it? Why don't we, for just this morning, put all these difficulties aside and go to church." She'd deal with her new Tony theories tomorrow.

He nodded. "I am glad it's Sunday."

Repentance notwithstanding, Liz enjoyed the service even more than usual. The current insanity of her world had not changed, but she found a refuge there in forgiveness and strength far greater than her own. Mr. Whittington, too, seemed to savor the songs, prayers, and Pastor Brad's sermon on Jesus raising Lazarus when all hope seemed lost.

After church, the old gentleman took a nap. Liz picked up a plate of rotisserie chicken and carried it, along with fruit and water, to her favorite backyard retreat—a bench shaded by big lilac bushes with a view of Jaynes Lake. Even in August, lake breezes found her there.

Liz feasted on food, landscape, and solitude. Returning to the inn, she found a note on her door from Mr. Whittington. He was leaving and would not return for coffee hour. Liz turned off both cell and landline, hitting the sofa for a long, lovely nap herself.

Waking up and stretching, she wondered what she would do with an entire delicious evening to herself.

But she didn't want to spend it alone. Aunt Ruth probably would be home, perhaps Miriam as well.

When her smiling aunt waved frantically from the front porch of her *Grossdawdy Haus*, Liz was doubly glad she'd chosen to visit her. Aunt Ruth reminded her so much of her late mother.

Her aunt had recovered well from an intruder's attack last fall, when she'd attempted to help Liz solve a case—which was why Liz had not asked her to help with Mr. Whittington's quest. Her face now beamed under her black Kapp, the picture of serenity, and Liz wanted to ensure she stayed that way.

While rocking, chatting, and eating shoofly pie, Liz could pretend she was a child again—though her childhood had been spent in Boston, far from her Amish roots.

Ruth's daughters, Phoebe and Tabitha, and their families dropped by, and soon the porch was filled with Swiss and English chatter and lots of yodeling.

Much as she enjoyed her family, Liz had never learned to like yodeling. That, plus her real desire to see Miriam, signaled an end to the visit. She drove slowly toward her cousin's farm, encountering several buggies, as the Amish often spent Sunday afternoons visiting relatives and friends.

Between houses, a small wiggle of unease crawled up Liz's back like a bug. The closer it crept to her mind, the bigger it grew.

She'd felt that way the day Bingo Guy, dressed as a businessman, appeared at a pedestrian crossing downtown. Liz peered in her mirrors. No one followed her. She looked across flat green-yellow soybean fields, where one could see roads a mile away. Another buggy or two. A truck turning in the opposite direction. Nothing that should upset her.

Maybe the burglary last night had spooked her more than she

realized. Surely, a fun Sunday evening with Miriam and Philip and their family would rid her of her unease.

But when she turned into Miriam's driveway, nobody sat on the porch. Liz rapped at the door, but no one answered.

Her nervousness returned with a vengeance. Going back to the quiet inn didn't seem like a good solution.

The sun still shone well above the horizon. Should she visit Uncle Amos and his brood?

Liz hesitated. Though she loved him and his family, the wall of reserve between them remained. A casual drop-in visit would make them all uncomfortable.

As she paused at the end of Miriam's driveway, Liz realized Lydia's farm was located maybe ten miles up the road.

How had the young woman coped since that awful burglary? In the back of her mind, Liz heard Chief Houghton warning her to stay away from the victims. However, without phone service, email, Facebook—she had no idea if Lydia was recovering or struggling to get out of bed each morning.

Maybe reassuring someone else was the best way to deal with her own fears.

Liz turned right and headed toward Lydia's house.

The sense of being watched followed her as if her stalker had hitched a wagon to her car. Again and again, she checked mirrors. A buggy here. A car there. And fields that seemed to stretch forever toward the setting sun.

Maybe she should keep binoculars in her car, as nosy Sadie did—ostensibly for birdwatching, but Liz knew better. Her edginess grew until her fingers trembled.

Honestly, Liz, get hold of yourself. Lydia didn't need a visitor who was jumping at shadows.

Liz turned off on a side road and headed back toward Pleasant Creek, watching for any change in other drivers' routes. One car a quarter mile behind her also turned off on her side road. But when Liz turned again, it continued on.

She was passing cornfields now, and six- and seven-foot cornstalks hid the view much more than soybean vines. A buggy here, another there drove behind her, toward her—of course, they all looked alike.

She lost her nerve. Better that she simply keep her eyes on the road and go home.

When she stopped at a station for gas, she called Jackson.

"Hi," he said, before she opened her mouth. "Want some company?"

"How did you know?" she asked, surprised. "Yes, I could use some—if you promise to stay awake. When Beans watches TV with me, he always falls asleep."

"I can do that." Jackson hung up before she could change her mind. Not that she wanted to.

Liz replaced the gas cap and drove to her inn that once more seemed like a haven.

When she awoke the next morning, her first thought was that she hoped Mr. Whittington had spent a fun, relaxing day yesterday.

Liz had enjoyed a laid-back evening watching useless TV with Jackson and afterward had even slept most of the night. And later this morning—hip-hip-hooray!—the air-conditioning repairman would come.

After the tensions she and Mr. Whittington had experienced the past two weeks, perhaps they could share a pleasant breakfast together.

Instead, he appeared preoccupied.

More than preoccupied. His mouth turned down, and large

wrinkles had taken up residence on his forehead. He didn't seem to notice she'd made the rosemary ham and cheese quiche he'd liked so much the week before.

Had he and Sadie quarreled? *Please, God, no. Give me one morning without drama between Mr. Whittington and a lady.*

When he let his tea grow cold, she nudged him. "Are you all right?"

He started. "Oh . . . I am fine, other than I did not sleep particularly well last night."

"Not unusual after a burglary." Plus, the man was past eighty. "Did you have a good time yesterday?"

His face lit with his first smile of the morning. "Sadie and I rode a roller coaster at a county fair and ate entirely too much cotton candy."

"No wonder you're not hungry."

Cyrus looked down at his nearly untouched quiche. "I haven't done your lovely breakfast justice, have I? We simply can't have that."

He ate more than half his large piece, but then said he had to take care of some business and left.

Having tabled her investigation of Tony on Sunday, she was eager to pursue it today—and perhaps reach a resolution that would settle her doubts. Liz called Tony's cell phone and left a message on his voice mail.

Curbing her impatience, she threw herself into stripping beds and doing laundry. Realizing she'd significantly depleted staples in her pantry, Liz drove to a grocery a few blocks off Main Street. Jackson called while she was standing in line at the checkout.

When she walked through the automatic door, still talking to him, she nearly ran her cart into him. "What are you doing here?"

He continued talking to her through his phone. "Just happened by and thought I would help lug your groceries to the car."

She kept her tone light, despite being a little annoyed. "Is this part of your keep-Liz-safe program?"

Maybe she shouldn't have called him last night.

"Of course. Grocery-lugging is a perk listed in our contract's fine print." He really did help, lifting heavy bags of charcoal and Beans's dog chow, chattering all the time.

Liz didn't pay much attention, though, because she caught sight of Mr. Whittington's top hat, then a glimpse of the man himself, walking down a nearby street. He was with someone, but she couldn't see his companion clearly.

Jackson could. "Wow. How many women does that guy date? This one looks extra young."

Liz asked, "You haven't seen her before?"

"No. Definitely from out of town."

Mr. Whittington didn't look happy. In fact, he seemed to have gone downhill since breakfast. The woman had turned toward him. She was talking in a low voice, and Liz couldn't see her face, but her slim hand stabbed a finger at the old gentleman again and again. Her sleek dark hair, striped with magenta and purple, curved in a trendy style that seemed familiar—

The courthouse researcher.

Liz strode, then jogged toward them, Jackson in her wake. "Liz, where are you going?"

At the sound of their approach, the girl slipped away and disappeared around a corner. Liz ran after her, Jackson following, but again, her quarry seemed to have vanished into thin air.

Panting, she pointed. "Jackson, will you look down that street? And that one? Call Houghton if you see the girl."

Though bewildered, he dashed away while Liz searched other streets.

She saw only an elderly man walking his dog. A mother pushing a baby in a stroller.

As she hurried back toward the parking lot, Liz called Jackson, but he hadn't spotted the girl either. "Thanks—and sorry, I'll explain later. I'm going back to talk to Mr. Whittington."

She hung up and broke into a dead run again, but the old gentleman also had disappeared.

As Liz peered into nearby alleys, Jackson overtook her, his face stern. "You want to tell me what this is all about?"

Feeling a little foolish, she found she didn't want to tell him at all. Still, Jackson certainly deserved an explanation of Liz's suspicions. "Would you mind talking about this in my car? Once there, I'll call the chief. Then I'll try to describe what I think is going on to both of you."

"Sure."

He accompanied her to her Acura and listened while she told Houghton what they had seen.

"Hmm. So Whittington does know that girl," the chief mused. "I'll have Hughes and Gerst look for her."

"I also wanted to let him know about the fingerprints in his room. We only found his, yours, and Sarah's. No matches in our criminal database. The intruder must have worn gloves." Houghton asked Liz to notify him when she saw Mr. Whittington again.

Liz agreed to call and hung up. She told Jackson the details of her encounter with the girl at the courthouse.

He hesitated. "Liz, I know you like Cyrus Whittington, but all the trouble seemed to start when he showed up."

When Tony showed up too. "You mean Mr. Whittington stole his own tea set?"

"How do we know it's his? All that valuable glass in his room could be stolen." Jackson's amiable gaze had hardened. "He's stuck around here a long time, hasn't he? He could be checking out local homes and businesses—who'd suspect a friendly old man?—then reporting to some outside person or persons. Like that woman, for instance."

"But ransacking Amish farms? That doesn't fit," Liz protested. "Plus, I'm sure you know about Gideon Sommer's arrest for vandalizing the Wickey farm."

"True." He ran his fingers through his thick hair. "Lots of things don't fit."

She fell back against the seat and moaned. "Too many snarls. Too many loose ends."

"Not a great way to start a week." Jackson patted her arm. "Wish I could do more to help you than haul bags of dog chow."

"You've done so much more than that." She let gratitude shine from her eyes.

He flashed his irresistible smile, and she could have sworn his cheeks pinked slightly. "Well, I'd love to chase a few more iffy criminals around town for you, but I probably should go back to work."

She laughed and checked her watch. "Me too. I actually have an air-conditioning guy coming soon."

"At least, that's something to celebrate." He high-fived her. "Keep me posted if anything comes up, and I'll call you later."

"Thanks, again." She waved and drove off, glad to escape his magnetism.

But also very glad she would talk to him tonight.

———— ⁄⁄⁄⁄⁄⁄⁄⁄⁄⁄⁄⁄⁄⁄⁄ ————

With groceries put away and the repairman come and gone, Liz would have loved to put her feet up and simply luxuriate in the inn's blessed coolness.

Nagging questions about Tony, however, would not let her mind rest. Since returning to the inn, she'd called him a couple of times, still reaching only his voice mail. Now Liz sat in the library with her laptop, researching the Charlotte, Michigan home address he'd given her when he checked in. Tony lived in Lakeview Apartments, so she called the manager's number. More voice mail.

Leaving messages didn't do much to answer her doubts. Liz searched online until she nailed down several phone numbers that matched the Lakeview Apartments address.

The first had been disconnected.

She called the next. "Hello, my name is Liz Eckardt, and I'm trying to contact Tony Lanham—"

Click.

The man that answered when she called the next number questioned Liz as if she were a suspect. "I don't know any Liz Eckardt. Who are you? Who's Tony Lanham? Why are you calling me? Where did you get my number?"

She couldn't edge in another word before he hung up.

Two more calls generated civil replies, but no, they didn't know a Tony Lanham.

When another landline owner went into a tirade against tele-marketers, Liz almost decided she'd done enough research for now.

She persisted through several more, however, and when an elderly woman's soft voice responded, "Tony Lanham? He's my neighbor," Liz's pulse quickened.

With a twinge of conscience niggling her, she fibbed, "Mr. Lanham stayed at my bed-and-breakfast recently, and I've been trying to contact him about possessions he may have left behind."

"Oh dear. I wish I could help you," the woman clucked her tongue. "And I so wish Tony still lived next door. He was such a nice young man, always dropping by to ask me if I needed anything."

"He no longer lives in Lakeview Apartments?"

"No, dear. He seems to have moved out in quite a hurry, without a word to anyone. Very unlike him."

Liz thanked the lady for her help, then called the Lakeview Apartments manager again. This time, a terse voice answered. Yes, Tony Lanham had moved. No, he had not left a forwarding address.

Perhaps she could reach him at his workplace. Liz called Tony's company, Apex Appliances, and repeated her possessions-left-behind speech to a secretary.

The woman answered, "I'm sorry. No Tony Lanham is employed here."

"You're sure?"

"Quite sure. Have a good day."

Liz stared at her phone. He'd lied about working there? Then Tony must have lied about the so-called work-related meetings that had brought him to Indiana. To the Olde Mansion Inn.

Perhaps he was indeed the kind of person who had to move out in a hurry, leaving no forwarding address.

But was he the kind of person who would steal an old man's tea set?

Maybe Tony was a "nice" person, beloved by naïve old ladies and clueless bulldogs. A "nice" person who would partner with a "nice" old man, a mean young woman, and a disguise freak to steal costly glass and other valuables?

Maybe they all hated Amish farmers too.

And innkeepers with blue-flowered china.

Liz fell back against the cushy chair.

Research was supposed to clarify cloudy issues.

Instead, these issues had coalesced into a senseless storm that seemed to have no end.

16

After Liz reported her findings regarding Tony to a surprised Chief Houghton, she dealt with her frustrations by scrubbing the oven to shiny, stainless steel perfection.

Then, to lift her mood, Liz decided to celebrate the inn's renewed coolness by baking fresh cookies for coffee hour, rather than raiding her emergency freezer stash. She'd invite Sadie and Mary Ann to brighten the day for Mr. Whittington, as well as herself.

Liz poked her head inside Sew Welcome's door. "Anybody up for warm oatmeal-cranberry-macadamia nut cookies at coffee hour?"

Mary Ann looked up from organizing a shelf. "I'd love some. Sadie will too, if she gets back from her errands before coffee hour."

"I'm sure Mr. Whittington would enjoy your company. He's had a rough time since the tea set theft."

Mary Ann gave her a quizzical look. "True. Still, you can't solve his every problem, Liz."

"Do you think I do more for him than I have for other guests? Other than the Brumpetts, that is."

Mary Ann rolled her eyes. "You went the hundredth mile with those two. But there's more to Mr. Cyrus Whittington than meets the eye."

A repeat of Jackson's opinion. Were they right?

Two customers entered and asked about quilting tools and notions. As Mary Ann directed them to the quilting area, Liz pulled up a stool behind the counter and pondered her friend's words.

As a businessman and mayor, Jackson dealt with people very well.

And Mary Ann, with decades of extensive community experience, really knew her stuff. If anyone could read a person, it was one of these two.

On the other hand, Liz's instincts told her Mr. Whittington truly was a kindly, charming old man.

But the same instincts had echoed similar sentiments regarding Tony. She'd check Mr. Whittington out on the Internet this evening.

That decided, she watched Mary Ann do what she did so well. Her friend's knowledge on a broad range of subjects was unparalleled.

Liz blinked. She'd faulted Houghton for not asking Mary Ann about the Wickey versus Sommer feud. Perhaps if she told her friend about Mr. Whittington's tea set mission, Mary Ann—the area's expert on the English and Amish—might fill in some blanks.

The customers selected a few items, paid, and left.

Liz relaunched their conversation. "Mr. Whittington did tell me more about his background—and his purpose for being here—than he's told everyone else."

"Yes, he informed Sadie he was looking for family."

"Good. Now I don't feel like I'm betraying his confidence. I would appreciate it if you'd keep this conversation between us, though." With her friend's nod of agreement, Liz continued, "I did research for him at the courthouse, but hit a wall." She reminded Mary Ann of Addie's mention of a tea set, then told of her own attempts at tracing Lydia King's parentage and her difficulty in nailing down Priscilla Glick's maiden name. "If I'd found Priscilla's name was Hertzler, that would have identified her as Cyrus's half sister, proving Lydia was descended from Priscilla."

Sure enough, Mary Ann's dark eyes flickered. "Priscilla Glick—quite an elderly lady. In her nineties, I think, when she died. I knew her daughter Eunice, who cared for her."

Of course Mary Ann knew Priscilla. Mary Ann knew everyone.

And Eunice. Another name she'd found in the Esh-Glick line. "Do you, by any chance, know Priscilla's maiden name?"

Her friend frowned. Liz could almost see the Mary Ann Berne search engine sorting and selecting at top speed.

She shook her head. "I don't think anyone ever mentioned it."

Liz's high dropped to a medium. "Could you put me in contact with Eunice? She seems to have disappeared off the face of the earth."

"Actually, she has. Eunice died not long after her mother did."

"Oh." Liz couldn't catch a genealogy break for anything.

"And Henry Esh, her son who lives in this area—"

"Lydia's father?" Liz perked up.

"Yes. But Henry and his wife thoroughly disapprove of the English. They won't be any help at all."

Oh, yes. Lydia's strict parents. Liz sighed.

"I do remember, though . . ." Mary Ann pressed her forehead.

What? What? Liz covered her mouth to keep from ruining her friend's concentration.

Mary Ann's face lit. "During a couple of visits, I remember Priscilla's repeating again and again that she wanted her teapot."

Liz's heart boomed bass drum beats. But was this clue enough to tell Mr. Whittington?

"That may not be sufficient to identify her as Cyrus's sister," Mary Ann lamented. "I wish I remembered her maiden name."

With Addie King's vague tea set clue and her great-great-grandmother's vague teapot clue, should Liz wait until she found stronger evidence for their kinship?

Liz's thoughts conducted a furious debate until coffee hour. Should she tell him? Given his emotional state right now, he didn't need more disappointments. On the other hand, shouldn't she keep him in the loop concerning potential progress in her search for his family?

The decision was made for her. Though Sadie returned in time to eat fresh-baked cookies, Mr. Whittington did not.

Sadie's nose turned red, which it often did when she was annoyed. "He could have at least let you know he wasn't coming."

Sadie probably was more irritated because Mr. Whittington had stood her up, but his thoughtlessness triggered a red flag in Liz's mind. "It's not like him."

He did not appear after dinner either. Since she was already thinking about Mr. Whittington, Liz opened her laptop to check him out online. Placing her fingers on the keys, she realized he'd told various people he'd worked in the glass industry, but never mentioned a specific company. She didn't even know if his company still existed. So she searched his name and found very little. She hadn't expected to find anything on social media, and she didn't. In his eighties, Mr. Whittington probably had retired twenty years ago, so no job connections showed up.

She did find brief funeral notices for his wife, Marilyn, and daughter, Sherry, in the archives of the *Philadelphia Inquirer*. Both had been lovely, and Sherry had inherited her father's million-dollar smile. Sherry had passed away in 1986, Marilyn in 2000. Despite Liz's doubts about the lonely octogenarian, she hoped that somehow, she could help him find the rest of his family.

Mr. Whittington remained absent even past his usual bedtime. She was on the verge of calling Houghton when the old gentleman showed up, so pale and grim she only wanted to help him upstairs to bed.

When she let Beans out early the next morning, his car was already gone.

Blast. The clock tower's serene chiming at the half hour seemed out of place. Where had Mr. Whittington gone?

"Liz, there's no law that forces him to tell you his plans." Mary

Ann, who'd come early to Sew Welcome, added gently, "No one expects you to watch over Mr. Whittington's every move."

"I know."

She went about her business, but in her mind, Liz paced.

The cup-smasher called again and broke more china in her ear. Liz slammed down the phone and jotted down the number her stalker had used this time.

That made up her mind. She didn't know what was coming to a head regarding Mr. Whittington, but some crisis had occurred, or was about to. If she could tell him she'd found his half sister's descendant, perhaps that would make a difference. Regardless, she had to do *something*. Something besides reporting another stupid phone call to Houghton. It was probably another untraceable disposable phone anyway.

After Liz scarfed a chicken salad sandwich for lunch, she jumped into her car and drove to Lydia and Dale's farm, ignoring every weird feeling that assailed her. What would she say when she arrived? Liz rehearsed half a dozen approaches, none of which seemed to make sense.

She pulled into their driveway. The late-afternoon sun sent lazy rays to sweep the summer landscape. Birds sang in big sycamores surrounding their house. Who would have thought that less than three weeks ago, vicious vandals had invaded this tranquil scene?

Addie bounced out the screen door, followed by Lydia. The young woman was still too pale, but looked much better nevertheless. She smiled and patted a straight chair on her porch. "Please, come sit with me."

Addie endured as much conversation as she could before running out to play with a tail-wagging puppy under the trees.

Liz patted her friend's arm. "I hope things are looking up for you."

"Thanks to family and friends, most of the damage has been repaired. I wish I could bounce back as Addie has." A genuine smile warmed Lydia's face as she watched her daughter. "I am glad she has recovered so well."

When their conversation returned to chitchat level, Liz told Lydia she'd been researching genealogies of area families for a friend and that currently, she was tracing the Glicks.

"But I'm finding large gaps in courthouse records." Liz tried to keep her voice casual. "I heard through the grapevine that you were related to them."

"I am." Lydia smiled again. "My *Grossmutter*—her name was Eunice—was a Glick; she was so special to me." Her blue eyes clouded a little. "I wish she could see Addie now."

"I'm sure she would have loved her." Wishing this were only a social visit, Liz pressed on. "I wondered if you could tell me about Priscilla Glick, your great-grandmother. My research hit a wall because I can't find her maiden name."

"I only knew her when she'd grown elderly and confused. Grossmutter loved her Mutter very much and took good care of her. What was her name?" Lydia frowned. "Heugin? Herschler? No. But I am sure it is in our family Bible."

She motioned Liz inside, asking if she wanted anything to drink.

Liz, trying not to dance with impatience, declined. As Lydia leafed through the typical large, plain German Bible, Liz glanced around the simple room. So tidy, with everything put back into place.

When Lydia pointed to an entry on a family record page and said, "Hertzler! I knew it began with an *H*!"

Gazing into Lydia's triumphant face, Liz wondered if the knowledge she now held might upset Lydia's world worse than a vicious burglary.

17

"Thanks for checking on that for me," Liz told Lydia as they returned to the porch and sat. "That will help my friend so much. It confirms he has family in this area he didn't know about. He is elderly, and his wife and only daughter are dead. So finding relations is especially important to him."

"I am glad to help."

What to say now? Lydia didn't appear to connect Mr. Whittington's search with herself.

Should Liz say anything? Wasn't this his affair? How could she decide how his secret should be handled?

She pictured him showing up at Lydia's out of the blue, not only an unknown English man, but one wearing a purple zebra-print T-shirt and orange pants, plus his ever-present slippers and top hat. The young Amish woman would slam the door in his face before he spoke a word.

Liz cleared her throat. "Lydia, actually, my friend, Cyrus Whittington—and yes, he is English—appears to be the younger half brother of your great-grandmother, Priscilla Hertzler." She looked into Lydia's quizzical face. "He only learned of her existence two years ago and was deeply saddened to discover she'd passed on. Since then, he has searched for Priscilla's descendants. He moved to Indiana from Philadelphia in hopes of finding and meeting perhaps the only family he has left."

No curiosity livened Lydia's eyes. Instead, she'd drawn slightly away from Liz. "No one in my family has ever mentioned such a thing."

"He brought with him a tea set," Liz pressed on, "one his father,

James Whittington, had made, similar to one he had made earlier for his daughter, Priscilla—your great-grandmother."

At the words "tea set," Lydia stiffened. "I . . . would rather not meet him."

Liz's heart sank. *Leave that subject alone.* She returned to her original approach. "I know this is a terrible time to surprise you like this. But Cyrus is in his eighties. Who knows how long he will live?" *Especially if he stays so upset.*

But Lydia's eyes had narrowed, her face whitened again. "No Whittington is listed in our Bible. He cannot be related to us." She shook her head firmly. "Tell him I will not meet with him, nor will my family."

Lydia stood.

Reluctantly, Liz did too. *I did my best, Mr. Whittington. But it wasn't enough.*

"I am sorry, Liz, but I have much to do this evening."

Liz bit her lip. "I'm sorry to have upset you, Lydia. I hope you will forgive me."

"Of course."

Her Amish faith demanded such forgiveness, but Lydia sounded cold. Now Liz ached for their budding friendship as the young woman turned and went into her house without so much as a good-bye.

But would her own pain begin to approach that of the old gentleman whose quest might have come to a heartrending end?

———— //////////////////////// ————

Since she already felt miserable, Liz decided she might as well tally up the month's bills. Hiding in her quarters from Mr. Whittington was a coward's way out, but she told herself she needed time before facing him at coffee hour.

Her often obstinate laptop, sensing her mood, threw tantrums that took her an hour to fix. She'd just coaxed it back to normalcy when her landline rang.

It might be a guest for next weekend—a welcome interruption, with only one reservation on the calendar. Liz moved toward the phone. But if that psycho cup-smasher was calling again—in passing, she grabbed her whistle from a junk drawer.

It was Lydia.

Her friend, who did not own a phone, had called her? Liz's heart warmed—

"I told you I did *not* want to see Whittington." Lydia's words shot through her like bullets. "Why did you send him here?"

Me? Her stomach and her mouth wobbled. "I—um—"

"I do not want to know him! I do not want his millions! Why can he not understand?"

"I don't know what you're talking about, Lydia. And I didn't—"

"Liz, if that *früt* Englishman sets foot on our property again—or if you do—Dale will call the police. Do you understand?"

Click.

Liz stared stupidly at the phone, still grasping the whistle in her paralyzed hand.

Finally, she hung up, dropped the whistle into the drawer, and sat on her sofa.

How had Mr. Whittington tracked down Lydia? Evidently his research had paid off too.

The past couple of weeks, she'd often sensed someone following her. But the thought had never occurred to her that it might be Mr. Whittington.

Numbly, she prepared for coffee hour, though she doubted he'd come.

He didn't.

That evening, she arrived at the Material Girls' quilting session, needing their support.

Sadie was busily organizing supplies with Mary Ann, so Mr. Whittington wasn't with her. Liz's mood hit a new low.

Naomi, entering with a tray of chocolate cupcakes, took one look at Liz and set down the tray. "What is it, Liz? What's going on?"

Mary Ann and Sadie ceased organizing. Caitlyn and Opal had just entered, but they, too, gathered around Liz as she sat in a rocker.

Liz told them everything. About Mr. Whittington's mission. About Lydia's caustic rejection of both him and Liz. About Lydia's bizarre comment about not wanting his millions.

"He told me he had some money," Sadie said slowly, "but that kind of money?"

"How can he possibly be a millionaire?" Liz thumped the rocker's arm. "I checked on him online, and almost nothing showed up. Wouldn't I find articles, even if somewhat dated, about his company, his social life, his charities? All I could find were his wife's and daughter's funeral notices, which told very little about his family."

Opal pursed her lips. "Maybe he has good reasons for not flaunting it."

"Or simply didn't want to make a big deal out of it," Sadie crossed her arms. "He may like Reg and expensive glass, but he also loves crazy secondhand clothes, county fairs, and cheap gas. He doesn't want to act like all the other millionaires. He wants to be himself."

Caitlyn hesitated. "Or—I hate to say this—Cyrus may be feeding Lydia a line. Maybe a line he's been feeding other people. You know, some scam in which they'll receive a fortune if they invest a few thousand dollars."

"But why move all the way to Indiana to fleece people here?" Liz shook her head. "And if he were targeting the Amish, he could have found plenty in Pennsylvania."

"Con men do move from one state to another to escape the authorities," Mary Ann said quietly.

"Maybe." Liz gripped her now-pounding head.

"I wish Mr. Whittington were here," Naomi said. "If only we could ask him our questions."

"I'd like that too." Liz's hand dropped. She raised her chin. "Until we can, I think we should consider him innocent until proven guilty."

"Hear, hear!" Sadie pumped her fist.

Mary Ann glanced around the room. "We're all agreed? Good. Let's work some more on this pumpkin quilt and hope Cyrus shows up."

With work to do on their project, fingers flew, and the usual hum of conversation arose. Liz's spirits lifted. *Amazing how working together to make something beautiful eases our stress.*

Cutting, basting, and piecing bits of fabric into the whimsical pumpkin patch under a starry sky, the Material Girls morphed their session into one of their most productive. They stretched it a half hour longer, hoping Mr. Whittington would walk through the door and charm them out of a cupcake or two.

Finally, though, Mary Ann called it quits, and they cleaned up.

"You call it quits too." She wagged a finger at Liz. "Don't wait up for him. Go to bed."

Liz thought she would lie awake half the night, listening for Mr. Whittington and jumping with the old house's every creak. Exhausted by the difficult day, though, she almost fell asleep before she'd pulled her sheet up to her chin.

When she woke up the next morning to let Beans out, Liz felt so good that afterward, she flipped the bulldog a slice of bologna, one of his favorite treats.

But when she peered out toward the parking lot, Reg was gone.

Or had the car and its driver never returned last night?

Don't panic, Liz. Mr. Whittington's disastrous visit with Lydia and his possible deception would pose valid reasons for his going elsewhere to stay.

"If this guy's a millionaire for real," she told Beans, "a few possessions left behind wouldn't be a big deal."

Beans didn't think it a big deal either, as he'd traveled to Doggy Dreamland before she finished her sentence.

How she wished she could absorb even a smidgen of the canine's laid-back attitude. Though Liz attacked the weedy flower beds that morning—a task that usually left her too drained to stew—she couldn't keep her worries locked in the airtight compartment to which she'd assigned them. As she plunged into other tasks, they rose like nighttime specters, shaking her at the most mundane moments.

Mary Ann found Liz blinking back tears as she cleaned the garbage disposal.

"What's the matter?" Mary Ann encircled Liz with her arm. "Did something happen to Cyrus?"

"That's the problem! I don't know! He could be charming the daylights out of another naïve innkeeper in the next county, but I just don't know . . ."

"No, you don't. Even if you called every inn within a hundred miles, they wouldn't tell you he was there." Mary Ann's no-nonsense tone helped Liz pull it together. "But do you think that's where Cyrus is?"

Liz shook her head vehemently. "Something's wrong. That girl downtown, the tea set theft, the way Cyrus has acted the past few days, and now his leaving without a word . . . I have to believe he's in trouble. But if I call Houghton, he'll give me the person-has-to-be-gone-for-twenty-four-hours spiel."

"You last saw him at breakfast yesterday. That's close enough." Mary Ann picked up Liz's cell phone from a counter. "Call him."

Liz tapped speed-dial and clapped it to her ear. Mary Ann pointed at her watch, indicating she had a sewing lesson to teach, and threw a kiss as she left.

"Whittington's gone?" Houghton spat out the words. "That guy is nothing but trouble."

"He may simply have decided to stay elsewhere. But without taking his funny clothes, his glass collection, or his record player? They're special to him."

"When did you last hear from him?"

Liz told Houghton about Mr. Whittington's visit with Lydia, including her reaction to her alleged relative's bizarre claim to be a millionaire.

"Good grief, Liz. You do seem to attract the nutcases."

"I know." If only the very sane Fremonts would return to the inn and stay a year.

"I suppose, though, that we'd better be on the lookout for Whittington. If he's been conning us, I'll hit him with every charge I can dig up," the chief growled.

About to hang up, Liz remembered to report the second cup-smasher call.

"Another one?" He whistled. "This guy's getting bold. And mean."

Had the caller been a guy? Liz paused. The calls featuring a male voice—sure. But smashing dishes seemed more like something a woman would do . . . which reminded her of Mr. Whittington's unhappy downtown rendezvous with the courthouse woman. Was she involved in all this? Liz related the incident to Houghton.

"Jackson already told me," the chief grunted. "Sounds like Whittington could be connected to some bad out-of-town types."

So far, this call hadn't improved her day.

Houghton said, "Oh, before I forget, I found out more about the Amish break-ins. The Sommer burglary appears to be a payback for the Wickey burglary. But Laban didn't instigate that vandalism to the Sommer farm."

"Who did?"

"Laban's younger brother, Ben."

Another young Amish kid in trouble. Liz sighed.

Houghton continued, "Ben had tried to recruit their cousin, Jonathan Wickey, to participate in Ben's revenge plans for Gideon's vandalism. Jonathan refused, but he couldn't bear the guilt in knowing about it. He came to see me last night."

"I guess you were right about the Amish conscience." The truth had come to light, but how sad that two families would continue to suffer.

"Usually comes through in one form or another." The chief didn't sound happy either.

"Has anyone admitted to the Kings' burglary? Or to taking Mr. Whittington's tea set?"

"The Wickeys and Sommers both deny vandalizing the Kings." He snorted. "When I asked the boys about the tea set, they looked at me as if I was crazy, so I'm pretty sure it's a separate incident, and the timing was actually coincidental. I think Whittington and that tea set are linked with some bad out-of-towners."

"I hope you're wrong." Her gut still told her Cyrus was in danger.

"We'll see." Houghton hung up.

Mary Ann and Sadie showed up for coffee hour, as if they knew Mr. Whittington wouldn't and that Liz would need their company.

Sadie had repeatedly called his cell number. "I'm so sick of talking to recordings I about threw my phone in the trash."

When Liz invited them to help check out Mr. Whittington's

favorite haunts after supper, Sadie jumped at the chance. Though his actions and lack of communication the past few days concerned her too, she shared Liz's conviction their friend was in trouble.

"I know the difference between good and bad men. Cyrus may have pulled a few shenanigans—like following you to find Lydia—but he's got a good heart," Sadie informed her. "Nobody can tell me different."

Wandering downtown, Liz marveled that, for once, the sense she was being followed seemed to have vanished. Did that mean Mr. Whittington had indeed been her only stalker?

They visited Mama's, the local drugstore, and the farmer's market. Though Liz didn't want to go to Harvey's Antiques, Sadie insisted.

"He loves their vintage clothes." Her eyes grew moist. "I bought him several bow ties there as a gift."

Harvey eyed them from afar and appeared relieved when they left. Liz explained to an insulted Sadie afterward why he didn't chat with them.

They covered River Road, their favorite scenic drive. The spectacular sunset's Midas touch, turning cornfields to gold, only added to their melancholy.

As purple twilight darkened the land, Liz turned back toward town. "Not many other places we can check tonight."

Sadie stared out the window. "No, I think we're done."

Liz hoped her friend would favor her with lame jokes on the way back. Sadie had been known to tell those at funerals if she thought they would cheer up her listeners.

But when she remained quiet, Liz tapped the radio, and they listened to music.

Both their phones rang as Liz pulled into the inn's parking lot.

"Guess we're popular," Sadie remarked as she picked up.

Liz turned off the Acura and answered hers.

The wave of horror that swept across Sadie's face drowned Liz's heart as Naomi said in her ear, "Thank God, you're all right. Sadie too?"

"Of course, we are. What's the matter?" Liz asked, but didn't want an answer.

"Dale King called the chief. Lydia's disappeared."

18

No. Not Lydia. Liz gasped, "Is Addie gone too?"

She closed her eyes, seeing the beautiful little pigtailed girl, playing with a puppy just this morning.

Naomi's "No, she's fine" was interrupted by Sadie's "No, she's okay."

Liz's limp brain didn't need a doubled-up conversation. She thanked Naomi and told her Sadie was probably talking to Mary Ann. Astute Naomi told her to call back if she needed to.

Liz had hoped to learn more details from listening to Sadie, but her friend was so furious, her end of the conversation didn't make much sense. Attempting to tune her out, Liz tried to recall the scanty facts she knew and list questions she wanted to ask.

Lydia had called her just yesterday afternoon, after Mr. Whittington saw her. When had she vanished? Had Lydia been gone overnight too?

Even in the shadows, Liz could see Sadie's nose had turned bright red. She hung up and smacked the dashboard almost hard enough to dent it. "I hate these—these—monsters!" Liz got the feeling that "monsters" was the tame version of what Sadie wanted to say. "They kidnap people and scare their kids to death. Poor Addie. Poor little Addie."

Nothing Liz could say expressed how mad she felt. She pounded the steering wheel, then gripped it until her fingers cracked.

Sadie slapped tears from her face and blew her nose. "Okay. What do we do first?"

"Well, for starters, let's go inside, and you can fill me in."

"Okay."

They headed for the kitchen and drank raspberry tea in the

breakfast nook while Sadie, now coherent, summarized Mary Ann's information. That afternoon Lydia had taken Addie with her to see the Simmons family, then left her child to stay overnight with her friends. Dale, who had been working in the field, came home for supper to find an empty house.

"He knew Lydia was visiting her friend," Sadie said, "but he'd expected her home by then. When more than an hour passed, he got worried and rode out to the Simmons place. He found she'd left more than three hours before, so he and Seth Simmons went to look for her."

Liz's temples tightened. "Did they find anything?"

"Lydia's horse and buggy tied several miles away, along a road she wouldn't have taken." Sadie shook her head. "No sign of Lydia anywhere."

Liz gritted her teeth. "I'm glad he called the police right away. Some of the Amish wouldn't have done that."

Sadie's nose reddened again. "To make things even worse, Dale thinks Cyrus abducted her. I know he disappeared too—"

"But I think the same person or persons who snatched Lydia kidnapped him first." Liz thumped her glass on the breakfast nook's table. "Remember that woman Jackson and I saw harassing him downtown? I just know she's got something to do with all this. I was thinking that a woman trying to intimidate another woman would be more likely to send broken china than a man. Remember that package I received? And those awful smashed-cup phone calls?"

"That works," Sadie agreed, "but I can't believe she'd do this alone. For one thing, Cyrus might be old, but he wouldn't let some girl kidnap him without putting up a fight."

"I wouldn't be surprised if Mean Girl joined forces with Bingo Guy. And possibly some other nasty people." Liz told her about Tony.

"Weirder and weirder." Sadie shook her head. "Why would they all take such risks?"

"Well, Houghton thought Cyrus was crazy or lying when he claimed to be a millionaire. But if that's true, then it's not hard to imagine these creeps found out. They're after him and any possible heirs." Liz pushed away her tea. "Anything else I should know?"

"I've told you everything Mary Ann told me." Sadie downed her last drops of tea.

Liz stood, fists clenched. "Then we have to get out there and look for Lydia. And for Mr. Whittington."

"Amen, sister." Her friend rose and started for the door. "Even if it takes all night."

———— *mmmmmmmmmmmmmmmm* ————

Recently, Liz had tried to make exercise a priority, and she'd lasted longer than she thought possible as she and the other Material Girls searched a large stretch of forest Houghton had assigned them.

But now, after hours of tramping through the woods, her sore feet tried to outshout her aching back for relief. She'd taken branches to the face until she learned to stay clear of Sadie, who pushed through underbrush as if leading an army.

Normally, Liz enjoyed hiking through the woods. But she hadn't done it at night since she'd thrown spooky Halloween parties for Steve's church youth group.

No party tonight. Not much of a moon either, and the stars were hiding. Mists drifted through the darkness, encircling trees as if to smother them.

Flashlights should have helped dispel the forest's eerie atmosphere, but seeing disembodied lights alternately bob and disappear in the distance only shot Liz's adrenaline through the sky. Who wielded the lights? What, if anything, had they found?

"What if we do corner those criminals?" Sadie had groused when

Houghton forbade her to bring her firearm. "Say, 'Please put down that gun and come with us to jail'?"

What indeed? At least Liz and her English friends possessed cell phones and pepper spray. A few Amish had borrowed phones, but what about the many Amish searchers who had none? What would they do if they encountered criminals with murder on their minds?

Liz tripped over a tree root and fell flat on her face.

Sadie crashed through the brush, blinding Liz with her flashlight. "You hurt?"

"Only my pride." *And maybe a rib or two.*

She dragged herself to her feet. *Lose the whining and the worries, Liz. Keep your mind on what you're doing.*

When she'd nearly covered her territory, Liz's phone dinged with a text. A group text from Houghton. Breathing a prayer, she checked it.

Found shed with Wickey colt, other stuff. No sign of LK or CW. Or perps.

The negative news made Liz want to sink to the ground. But Houghton's categorizing Cyrus with Lydia rather than with the kidnappers lifted Liz a little. Maybe Houghton still considered the possibility he was a victim too.

The chief hadn't mentioned the tea set. *No surprise there.* Apparently the shed housed only booty taken during the Wickey burglary.

While Liz searched her section of the woods, she'd reviewed the King incident. More than ever, Lydia's break-in appeared different in nature from the others—the intruders clearly were seeking something, not just being nasty. And though Liz's inn hadn't been damaged, the burglar had targeted Mr. Whittington's tea set. The two crimes fit together. Though Lydia hadn't admitted to owning a Whittington tea set, she'd disappeared when Mr. Whittington got too close for the criminals' comfort. Since the tea sets were tied to Mr. Whittington, they also had abducted him.

Why couldn't Houghton see it?

Though if she didn't focus, she might miss clues that could help find Lydia and the old gentleman. She forced her mind back to the task at hand.

When Liz and Sadie finished their sections, they texted Houghton and the other Material Girls. *Nothing here. Going home.*

Mary Ann replied, *Caitlyn and I almost done too. Hugs.*

Liz drove back to the inn in the inky emptiness of the night. Not bothering to undress, she dropped onto her bed. Her body shut down immediately, but her mind sent her crawling through tight, shadowy, vine-covered corridors all night.

The chief looks exhausted. Liz had never seen him look more fatigued as he prepared to address the large, tired group gathered outside the Kings' home. Mary Ann and Opal, who had been searching all morning, joined Liz and Sadie in a group hug that spoke everything they were too spent to say.

"Naomi and Caitlyn both had to work." Mary Ann, whose amazing hair always stayed in place, now pushed a straggly strand from her face. "But if the search continues tomorrow—"

"Shh. The chief's talking." Opal shushed Mary Ann and got away with it.

Liz, the Material Girls, and other searchers gathered closer, hoping to hear some inkling of good news that would fuel their afternoon.

"Thanks to all of you, we've covered a large area surrounding the spot where the buggy was discovered," Houghton said. "The state police with their K-9 units haven't found much yet. Followed Lydia's trail from the buggy, but it disappeared at the river. Haven't picked it up again—yet."

Dale sat with his brothers. He stared at his feet, expressionless.

Liz didn't dare look Dale in the eye because he linked her with Mr. Whittington. If only he could read her thoughts. Though she believed the old gentleman too had been kidnapped, her heart ached even more for the young man and his daughter.

Houghton cleared his throat. "Any trail Mr. Whittington might have left appears cold. No sign of his car either. In one way, that's good news. You don't see many cars like his coupe, and you don't see many guys who look like him. So I'd think they'll be easy to spot."

A few weak chuckles rose among the crowd, amid rumbles of anger from those who considered him a kidnapper. Sadie's mouth shriveled into a grimace.

The chief continued, "I put out an APB, circulating pictures of him and Lydia, plus his license plate number throughout Indiana and the rest of the Midwest. Hundreds of police officers have been on the lookout for him, which makes me think Whittington hasn't driven the car out of state. So we just gotta keep looking. We'll spread out more this afternoon to new areas, widen the search. Should find something soon."

Something? Liz swallowed. *Not someone?* And now, the chief made Mr. Whittington sound as if he were an escaped criminal. A criminal forcing Lydia to go with him?

"Right now, let's eat. Then I'd advise you to sack out for a little bit if you're going to look this afternoon, 'cause many of you haven't slept much. Thanks to all for your help. We—along with Dale and his family, I'm sure—appreciate you more than we can say."

Makeshift tables piled with food brought by Amish women and Mama's Home Cooking awaited.

Jackson, talking on his phone off to the side, waved to Liz. He'd been almost as inundated with calls as Houghton.

With her stomach contracted into a tight ball, Liz didn't think she'd eat much. But Doris Henderson, owner of Mama's Home Cooking, had sent her homemade chicken and noodles, and no one made pies like the Amish except Mary Ann. After the Material Girls ate, they set phone alarms for an hour's nap and, despite the heat, collapsed on their car seats.

Liz woke up sweaty, but somewhat refreshed. Sadie met her on the way to the line of searchers visiting the Kings' outdoor pump, where they guzzled water and filled their bottles.

Harvey, standing in line near Liz, studiously avoided looking at her. *I won't talk to you. I promise.*

"Mary Ann and Opal already have headed west," Sadie informed Liz. "But I've been thinking about one area nobody's searched yet. Maybe most people don't know about it."

"Well, no one knows this county like you do." Liz was glad to see color had returned to her friend's face.

"These woods aren't far from the Boy Scout camp, maybe fifteen miles north of town. Years ago, I was a den mother for our Cub Scout troop, and I helped with hikes there. Not a big forest, but it was pretty isolated, more rocky and rugged than most of Indiana. There were little caves there too—good hiding places. Much better than around here." She eyed Liz. "Didn't you say Bingo Guy wore hiking boots?"

Liz nodded, her heart beating faster. "Sounds like a good spot to check. C'mon, let's go tell Houghton."

How long had the chief gone without sleep? Between bags under his eyes and scrunched eyebrows, Liz couldn't see his eyes.

Houghton said, "You know this place, Sadie? I haven't been there."

"It's way off Rocky Road. Been a long time," Sadie admitted, "but

I explored every nook and cranny with the Scouts. I could find my way around there with my eyes shut."

The chief's phone rang and he paused to answer.

Liz tried not to fidget. Sadie openly tapped her toe.

Jackson, looking tired but fit, walked up. "Want to join my group? We're headed south."

"Sadie thinks we should look to the northeast."

The chief hung up. "Sorry." He frowned. "The Boy Scout camp's a ways away."

"Is that where you're going?" Now Jackson frowned.

Sadie sniffed. "We're not headed to Timbuktu, you know."

Jackson's group gestured to him, and reluctantly he left. "I'll call you later, Liz."

The thought of his call reassured her.

The chief watched him go. "I'd send someone with you, but a lot of people had to go home or back to work. My officers are stretched thin already."

"We'll call you every couple of hours," Liz promised.

"Well, okay. Keep in touch. We don't want to have to go looking for you too."

A state policeman approached Houghton, so they headed for Sadie's pink Jeep before the chief could change his mind.

Once out of his sight, Sadie made up for lost time, roaring through the countryside.

"This county is crawling with cops," Liz protested, "and they don't know you like the Pleasant Creek police do. This Jeep isn't exactly subtle. You want to get us stopped before we even start?"

"They won't bother with us," Sadie huffed. "They've got criminals to catch." But she dropped her speed. A little.

The terrain changed from flat fields to gentle swells, then to hills, with fewer houses. Sadie took country roads, careening the Jeep around curves.

Liz completely lost her sense of direction. "What a change in such a short time."

"Glad we got our hiking shoes on," Sadie said, "because we'll need 'em."

She whipped the Jeep off Rocky Road, seemingly into a field bordering a forest. Weeds and scrubby bushes brushed the Jeep's sides.

They thumped and bumped their way to a dead end.

"All out!" Sadie hopped out of the driver's side. "We'll walk from here."

Liz plunged into the woods behind Sadie. They'd handled underbrush earlier, but the trees here had grown close together, with thickets and tangled grapevines that blocked every move.

"It's grown up more than when we hiked here," Sadie said when they paused to rest. "Maybe they don't bring Scouts to these woods like they used to."

I sure hope you remember the landmarks, or even recognize them. The terrain had grown rockier, and now they encountered occasional trickles of water at the bottom of small gorges.

"Glad the weather's been dry," Sadie said, "Or we'd be sloshing through streams."

"I'm glad we're not doing this at night." Liz chugged water from her bottle. "But at least it's cooler here than out in the sun."

Sadie pointed. "See the little cave?"

Liz stooped and looked in. Dark, slimy, with water dripping from the ceiling. Mr. Whittington seemed vigorous for his age, but if he were being held in something like this . . .

"I know of a couple of larger ones, so that's where we're headed."

Liz lowered her voice. "This is an excellent hiding place. We probably should hike as quietly as possible."

"You're right." Sadie no longer charged through the underbrush. Instead, she slipped from tree to rock to cave—had she learned that from the Scouts?

The woman's stamina was amazing. But then, she'd done heavy farmwork all her life. Liz kept up with her, but she hoped the larger caves weren't too far away.

When they rested twenty minutes later, Liz pulled out her phone and pointed to it.

Sadie nodded, understanding she meant to contact Houghton. No service.

Liz shook her head. "I should have realized phone service would be spotty out here, at best."

Sadie whispered, "You'd probably get more bars if we climbed higher. Let's try this ridge, and maybe we'll get through."

The ridge proved steeper than Liz realized, both rocky and slippery. When they had nearly reached the top, Liz pulled out her phone again. Two bars. Not great, but it would do.

"I'll text him," she told Sadie. "Quieter than a call. And we won't interrupt him."

The pounding in her temples relaxed somewhat. They really needed to stay in contact with Houghton. She tapped out a short text and pocketed her phone again.

Sadie gestured down toward the gorge again, and they wound their way to their original route, trying to avoid noisy plunges down the hillside.

As they hiked, Sadie raised her head like a doe, as if listening. Liz strained for sounds other than the subdued birds' chirps, streams' murmurs, and the forest rustles of late afternoon.

"We're almost there," Sadie murmured.

"Take it slow." Liz pulled pepper spray from her backpack, readying it. Sadie did likewise, and they slipped from tree to tree, thicket to thicket, listening to the quiet.

When Sadie pointed, Liz saw nothing different in the terrain—a rocky, shady hillside, thick bushes, dense trees.

"Behind the bushes near the bottom of the hill," Sadie mouthed.

Sure enough, dark patches showed between branches. But unless an observer knew of the cave behind the thicket, she'd never suspect its existence.

Her gaze shifted to the surrounding area, searching for anything that didn't fit the tranquil scene. Any small flashes of color? Unusual movements?

Sadie's gaze flitted from tree to tree as well.

They waited.

A cardinal's whistle made them jump.

They crept till they almost reached the cave's mouth.

She heard a small sound, like a whimper.

Had she imagined it?

From Sadie's abrupt stop, her friend must have imagined it too.

Liz dropped to her knees and crawled into the thicket covering the cave. When Sadie attempted to follow, Liz turned and shook her head, pointing to the surrounding woods. "Stand guard," she mouthed.

Sadie frowned, but relief touched her features.

You might be tough, girl, but you are over seventy.

Sadie knelt behind a nearby shrub, but she shifted so she could monitor the woods.

As Liz crawled past the bushes, a small stream of air hit her face, cool as if someone had turned on an air conditioner. The gritty mud chilled her knees as she crept through the cave's narrow mouth and paused in the shadows. Her confused eyes tried to adjust to darkness.

An echoing, slow drip greeted her.

She heard a rustle in the deep gloom, but no whimper.

She had no idea how far back the cave went.

Or what awaited her there.

Or here? Even as she tried to blink clarity back to her vision, an assailant could be flattened against the cave walls.

Her right hand still grasped the pepper spray. With any luck, she'd only have to use it on snakes.

Every cell in her body longed to back out of this dank, claustrophobic prison. As her sight cleared, she saw that she was in a large, empty antechamber, with a small tunnel at the back that she'd have to crawl through. The cave devoured every ray of light it could grab. How long before she would *have* to use her flashlight or phone for light?

She slipped through the antechamber and crouched to slide into the tunnel. She pushed forward, knee-step by knee-step.

Her knees screaming now, Liz felt for a wall, and her fingers encountered a slimy one. *Ewww.* According to what she felt, the cave's height at this point was about three feet. Crouching would cramp her back and shoulders, but she could alternate it with crawling.

Knee-step. Knee-step. Knee-step. Knee-step. Crouch-move. Crouch-move. Crouch-*whack*!

Liz smothered a cry as pain exploded in her head. She pressed her scalp, trying to contain the hurt. *Uniform ceilings are not a given, Einstein-Eckardt.*

Liz crawled along the wall again. When she couldn't stand it anymore, she stood, bent like a sapling, and took another step forward to encounter a strange sensation.

A soft, warm something struggled under her foot.

19

Liz smothered a scream at the same time the creature did.

As snakes did not scream, and assailants would have attacked, Liz knelt, turning on her phone.

Its glow revealed Lydia's terrified eyes in her quivering face, half-covered with a dirty gag.

Liz slipped it down.

The girl could speak only gasping, tearful Swiss as Liz turned on her flashlight and fought with knots in her bonds. After freeing Lydia, Liz beamed her flashlight throughout the small room. Nothing. No one.

She whispered, "Did they bring Cyrus here?"

Lydia nodded, her face trembling. "She took him."

They'd question Lydia later. Liz shoved her pepper spray into a pocket and aimed the flashlight. "Let's go."

Lydia stumbled. Liz supported her, but the passage was a tight, difficult fit for a side-by-side escape, crawl or crouch.

Slow it down for Lydia.

Run, run! He could be hurt . . . or worse!

Liz's instincts battled as dim light from the cave's narrow mouth tantalized every nerve.

Lydia, sobbing, streaked past Liz, charging through the cave's mouth. Liz followed on her heels, ready to hug Sadie within an inch of her life.

But her friend's startled, then terrified face halted Liz in her tracks.

A gun's muzzle jabbed her back.

"You just couldn't leave it alone, could you?"

———————— ⁓⁓⁓⁓⁓⁓⁓⁓⁓⁓⁓⁓⁓⁓ ————————

When he ordered her to stand beside Sadie, the sight of Bingo Guy's sneering face didn't surprise Liz.

Soundlessly, Lydia crumpled to the ground, her wet, filthy dress clinging to her. The young woman's shoulders shook, so Liz knew she hadn't fainted. She and Sadie knelt, trying to soothe the distraught girl.

Though a raging cloud mushroomed inside her, Liz commanded herself to keep cool. *Gather information. Find a way to beat this guy.*

Sadie's hunched shoulders, the emptiness in her face broke Liz's heart.

"Sorry," Sadie whispered. "I was watching for you to come out of the cave instead of keeping an actual lookout. He snuck up on me."

"Quiet!" Bingo Guy snapped.

Liz squeezed Sadie's hand. She ignored her own sinking heart to focus on their captor.

Apparently, when she and Mary Ann had encountered him, they'd caught Bingo Guy looking like himself—early twenties, wiry build, dark hair, and sharp features that could be handsome if enhanced by a genuine smile. He wore a ragged blue-and-white Columbia University T-shirt and shorts and carried a backpack. His feet, clad in hiking boots, turned in.

He held a big, ugly handgun.

Bingo Guy swore. "You should have minded your own business. Hand over your phones." He shoved them into his pockets and glared at Liz. "Your friend had pepper spray. Give me yours." Still training his revolver on them, he stuffed it into his pocket too.

Her ears caught an East Coast accent. Perhaps in disguising his voice over the phone, he'd modified it. She was sure she hadn't heard an accent during the phone calls. Then again, there hadn't been much actual speech.

"Throw your backpacks over there. You and the old lady, kneel with your hands over your head. Now."

They obeyed, but Liz couldn't stop herself. "Where have you taken Mr. Whittington?"

"Never mind about the old man. Maybe you'd better worry about yourselves."

He'd moved behind them. She couldn't see his face, but the hatred in his voice chilled her.

If only she hadn't texted Houghton right before they went to the cave. For at least another hour, he'd assume they were fine . . .

Something sailed over her shoulder and hit the ground in front of them. Rope.

She jumped, then froze as the gun prodded her back.

"Okay, smart lady, tie your friends' hands behind their backs. And don't try anything or they'll die, understand?"

Surely she was home in bed, having a nightmare. Because only in a nightmare would she tie up her friends.

The scratchy bonds, the warmth of Sadie's wrists as Liz knotted the ropes, and the clamminess of Lydia's skin shouted otherwise. The young mother lay on her side, still as death. Liz glanced several times to make sure she was breathing.

Liz had almost finished her hateful task when a series of rustles, grunts, and oaths behind her turned her head.

Mean Girl. Shoving a bleeding Mr. Whittington to the ground.

Liz's breath left her.

"About time you got here," Bingo Guy spat. "It took you half an hour to walk fifty feet?"

"It's not like your grandpa's ready for the Olympics." She nudged him with a foot.

Mr. Whittington was *his* grandfather?

"That's your fault." He glared.

She rolled her eyes. "Don't be a wuss, Ty. I had to make him talk. We have to do what we have to do."

"Shut up and help me get them into the cave."

"In a minute." For the first time, Mean Girl's gaze lit on Liz, and she slapped her hard across the face.

Even as Liz fell on her back, she saw Sadie's face darken, her posture stiffen as if ready to spring.

Don't.

Ty planted himself between the girl and Liz. "Chill, Kristen. We still need her. And the others."

For what?

For how long?

Kristen swore, but dragged Lydia to her feet. Sadie rose and propped the swaying Amish woman on the other side. Liz, slowly standing, understood her friend's survival instincts. They had to appease their captors' rage whenever possible.

Her gaze met Sadie's. *We just have to make it a little longer.*

Long enough for the chief to realize something was wrong and track them down.

Maybe by sunset? Yes, surely by sunset.

Having chalked that up as a given, Liz tried to reference their jailers' names: Kristen. Ty. No, she hadn't heard either recently . . .

Ty hauled his grandfather to his feet. The old man walked to the cave as if in a trance, his eyes glazed over.

Gritting her teeth to contain her inner volcano, Liz knelt and crawled through brush into the cave with the others. Their captors took turns holding them at gunpoint and binding them. Tyler, stronger than he looked, threw them all, like full trash bags, into the back of the cave.

A stony wall struck her back. Hard, gritty floor chafed Liz's bruised cheeks. The cave's dark twilight closed in on her, and for a while, she sensed only sharp rocks that gouged her sore body.

The sound of footsteps awakened her like a siren. Adrenaline pumped through her veins.

Was someone untying her ankles?

"Get up," Ty's voice snarled. His rough hand yanked on her arm. "We have business to take care of."

At least they were leaving the cave. Air and sunshine never felt so good, even if it might be the last she breathed on earth.

"Hurry back," Kristen growled. Sitting by the cave's mouth, she resumed eating her sandwich.

Liz's stomach growled too. Suppertime? She wasn't sure.

Ty pushed her ahead of him up a ridge. "Climb until I tell you to stop."

Her aching bones protested. But she did find his gun extremely motivating.

Two-thirds of the way up the ridge, he told her to halt. His gun—never moved from her as he glanced down and laughed. "Our mole's report, about an hour ago. Says when he left, they all were still wandering in circles."

These creeps had inside help? She choked.

Still leveling the pistol, he pulled out her phone. "Now it's your turn." He handed her the phone. "Put your password in."

She did, and he checked her screen.

"You've got texts, mostly from your boyfriend, the mayor. Type that you're okay and you'll see him later, then show me before you send." The gun touched her chin. "Understand?"

She nodded and obeyed.

"Now the chief needs to hear your voice. Call him, like you said you would."

"How do you know I said I'd call him?" she demanded.

"I was there. With the searchers," he sneered.

Her throat closed.

"Don't tell me you didn't see me." His smile morphed into another snarl. "After you and your weird friend spotted me by the lake as I was getting the lay of the land, I thought I was done for. With you solving mysteries before and knowing what I look like, I was sure this whole plan was down the tubes.

"But you didn't catch me this time," he crowed. "I found out where the police were looking. Where searchers were looking. All while playing a concerned citizen of Pleasant Creek, doing my civic duty."

His lurking among rescuers freaked her out even more. *Don't lose it, Liz. Don't let him win.*

"Now you're going to call your precious chief. You're going to pretend everything's fine, but you didn't find anything, and you're heading home. Let's see if you're as good an actor as I am."

He tapped her speed dial, then handed the phone to Liz and put his gun to her temple.

Breathe slow. Deep.

"So, nothing on your end, Liz?"

The chief's gravelly voice had never sounded so beautiful. She tried to steady her own. "No. We're beat. Anything on yours?"

"Nothing to speak of."

"We still have to hike back to the Jeep. Think we'll stop for dinner on the way home." *Nobody will discover we're missing until it's too late.*

"Liz, you'd better get moving. Shouldn't be there after dark."

"I know."

"Thanks again."

Click.

"Good job." The revolver moved from her head to her back.

She said nothing.

The sun's final light clung to Liz, then disappeared as they meandered down the ridge.

With it went her last hope for their sunset rescue, her "given" that had not been given at all.

20

Luckily Ty seemed preoccupied on the way back to the cave. Liz treaded as lightly as possible in the growing twilight—anything to keep his attention away from her.

Although, with a girlfriend like Kristen, Ty probably knew better than to extend their time away. Though not setting speed records, he was following her instructions to "hurry back."

Approaching the hidden entrance of the cave, Liz breathed a sigh of relief, hoping Ty wouldn't shoot her in front of the others. How weird to view the cave as a refuge.

Only the dimmest of lights illuminated its mouth behind the thicket's branches.

Liz stiffened as she heard not one, but two voices.

Kristen's, of course. But who else?

"Guard duty? You mean I have to stay the night here?" The man's voice rose almost to a squeak. "I've been hiking all day."

No, it wasn't Tony.

The mole.

Actually, the rabbit. *Harvey, no.*

Ty laughed again. "He's not very smart. But sometimes he's been useful."

"I didn't sign up for this." A note of rage invaded his whiny voice. "All I was supposed to do was deliver a package."

Ty shoved Liz through the thicket. She fell to her knees inside the entrance. Blinking, she saw Kristen and Harvey sitting on the cave floor, a small propane lantern casting shadows on their faces, the ceiling, and the walls. Her friends lay behind them like mummies.

Harvey glared as if his troubles were all her fault. "You and your stupid dishes. Why did you have to walk through my door?"

Even if answering hadn't involved risks, Liz wouldn't have bothered. *Pathetic. That's what you are.*

When Kristen spoke, her reasonable tone shocked Liz more than if she'd screeched at him. "Look, Harvey, I have a plan."

I'll bet you do. And it's probably good only for Kristen.

"We'll work this out. But maybe outside?" She gestured toward Liz. "Ty?"

Her boyfriend threw Liz into the back of the cave, bound her ankles, and gagged her again.

The three left, taking the lantern with them.

The murmur of their voices floated through the night, but Liz caught only a word here and there, "money" being the main one.

Of course.

Money had to be the subject of the conversation she'd witnessed from a distance between Mr. Whittington and Kristen, outside the grocery.

This was all about inheritance.

I understand now why you hated to leave your millions to Ty, Mr. Whittington. Is he Sherry's son? Or the child of another child you didn't mention?

If only she could hear what they were saying and try to counter Kristen's awful plan. If only she could stay awake, maybe roll closer . . .

Liz fought sleep, but her traitorous body was shutting down. Liz breathed a silent prayer for herself and her friends as darkness closed in.

———— ///////////////////// ————

Loud voices argued outside the cave.

Was it morning? Liz raised her heavy head.

"We have to move on this, Ty. They'll come looking for us today."

"I know. But I don't want . . . this."

"You're a wuss, Ty. This is the way it has to be." Kristen's sharp tones softened to persuasive. "Baby, we didn't plan it this way. But it's not like we have a choice now. And we'll be gone before the cops find them. Out of the country and on the way to our dreams."

Footsteps grated on the cave floor. Lantern light pierced the darkness.

I love you, Steve. God, please tell my godson I love him.

Ty and Kristen shoved the women aside and slid Mr. Whittington to a sitting position against the cave wall.

Were they to be forced to watch each other's murders?

Instead, Ty pulled down the old man's gag and placed a canteen to his lips.

Though Liz heard drips as water spilled, she also distinguished gurgles as he swallowed. *Good.*

"Here, Grandpa. Kristen fixed you a sandwich."

The old gentleman's eyes opened for the first time, glittering.

Liz caught her breath. Mr. Whittington, the charmer, the sweetheart, looked as if he wanted to spit in Ty's face.

But hunger won, and the captive chewed slowly, as if he'd forgotten how.

Liz trembled with rage. How long had they deprived him of food?

As Mr. Whittington ate, Ty crooned, "After this, I'll take you on my ATV so you won't have to walk. We'll go to my apartment for a hot shower. Then we'll contact your bank and talk to your favorite guy. After that, we'll visit my lawyer."

Eyes flashing again, the elderly millionaire said haltingly, "I'm not signing anything."

"Oh yes you will," Kristen broke in. "Because if you don't, your girlfriends here won't live too long."

The wrathful light in the old man's eyes died.

Liz choked. How could Kristen think he believed those lies? Mr. Whittington must know her casual pronouncement sealed death sentences for all, whether he surrendered to their demands or not.

But if he didn't give in, his jailers certainly would kill them all now, with zero chance of rescue.

Rescue. Had Naomi called her repeatedly, with no answer? Would Mary Ann realize Sadie was missing before she opened their shop at ten o'clock? And Jackson had been calling her every morning. Would he think it suspicious when she didn't answer today?

Ty and Kristen untied his grandfather and hoisted him to his feet, supporting him so he wouldn't topple. Liz wanted to mumble a good-bye as they helped him limp past, but she didn't want to make this harder for him.

Be strong, Mr. Whittington.

After they left, Liz rocked and fidgeted until she could touch Lydia. She gently rubbed the girl's back with the tips of two fingers.

Lydia stiffened, then relaxed. She murmured a faint something Liz couldn't decipher, but the tone said, "All is well between us."

Liz rolled to Sadie, who faced her. With the dim advent of morning light into the cave, she could see the outline of Sadie's trembling smile. Shifting and fumbling, they were able to join pinky fingers.

A light blinded her as if they lay on a Hollywood stage. "You two trying to pull something? Don't even think about it."

Kristen's words knifed through her. *Of course you don't comprehend love or friendship.* For the first time, a rivulet of pity trickled through Liz.

Something in her expression must have detonated Kristen's wrath. She shrieked, "For someone who's supposed to be so smart, you sure are dumb. I *wanted* you to stay out of this. Anyone else would have backed down when I had Harvey leave that package. When I smashed those cups over the phone. But no, you kept hanging around that antiques store and around Cyrus and Lydia, and then tramping all over the county to find us. You have only yourself to blame." She kicked Liz in the gut, hard.

Pain and nausea curled her into a tight spindle of agony, worsened by Sadie's cry as Kristen booted her in the back.

Kristen screamed at them, "Did you think I'd just wait for Ty to call? To give me permission?" She landed another vicious kick in Lydia's back. A metallic gleam shone in her hand. "I don't think so. You need to be taken care of now."

"What *you* think," said a deep voice behind her, "doesn't matter."

Tears washed down Liz's face, soaking her gag, but she didn't care.

"Drop the gun," Jackson said, "or I just might accidentally hit this trigger."

21

The second Jackson slipped the gag from her mouth, Liz pleaded, "Call Houghton. Ty—he says he's Cyrus's grandson—still has him!"

"One thing at a time." Jackson, still holding his gun on Kristen, kicked hers to the other side of the cave. He ordered Kristen to untie Liz. "Do it fast."

She swore at him, Liz, the ropes, the world, but she obeyed. Liz pointed Jackson's gun at Kristen while he tied and gagged her. The woman's eyes smoldered in the shadows like burning coals.

Jackson handed Liz a water bottle and his phone. "Actually, Houghton should be close by now. I was a Cub Scout in Sadie's den, so I beat him here. Should have come with you in the first place."

"You came when we needed you most." She tried to pour her gratitude into one look.

Jackson squeezed her hand. Then he began untying Sadie and Lydia while Liz, wary of an appearance by Harvey or Tyler, pointed his gun toward the cave entrance. When her friends were free, she handed the weapon back to Jackson before she clasped first Sadie, then Lydia in tearful hugs. But right now, every minute counted if Cyrus were to survive. "I need to call Houghton. And I'll have to go up on the ridge to do it."

Sadie fished a phone from Kristen's pocket. She picked up the woman's pistol from the floor. "Nice little number. I can handle this."

She pointed the gun at the woman with a not-very-nice smile. "I'm a crack shot, honey, so don't even blink." Sadie gestured with her head. "Take Liz up there, Jackson. I'll keep an eye out for any trouble here."

Lydia, who had obviously had enough of firearms, sank to the floor and leaned against the cave wall, closing her eyes. Patting the Amish woman's hand, Sadie aimed her glittering gaze and the gun toward the cave entrance.

God help you, Harvey, if you stick a toe into this cave.

Jackson steadied Liz as she stumbled through the dimness. They halted at the cave's entrance, listening.

Liz, on one side of the cavern, scoured the nearby hillside for unexplained movement. She cast an occasional glance at Jackson, standing on the opposite side. His fun, easygoing mayor persona had disappeared. Eyes narrowed in his taut face, he stared at the terrain as if reading it like a book.

When satisfied, they climbed the ridge, heads swiveling with every step. At the top, behind a thicket, Jackson handed Liz his phone.

So good to hear Houghton's voice. He didn't drown her with questions, just listened to her story. Though he did not raise his voice, she knew Harvey's involvement had caught him off guard too.

"He wasn't here this morning." A thin thread of fear spiraled up her back again. "I don't know where he's gone."

"Stay cautious until I get there," the chief said. "We'll follow up with Harvey. But right now, I'll contact the Fort Wayne police. If they can't track Whittington's bank immediately, I imagine they'll alert all the banks in the area."

"I think Kristen and Ty have changed tactics," Liz told him. "Originally, they planned to coerce Mr. Whittington into changing his will. Now, they just want to leave the country. I'm guessing they're forcing him to make a huge electronic transfer to an account Ty controls." She gave a light chuckle. "But his grandfather pays for everything in cash. As old-fashioned as he is, they may have to do something in person. Ty mentioned working with Mr. Whittington's 'favorite guy'—perhaps a bank officer. If they do, Ty may masquerade as his lawyer or investor. He can look amazingly respectable. I also imagine Ty's driving a different car by now. Maybe Kristen's or a rental." She rubbed her aching forehead. "I wish I knew her last name—though I imagine she's using an alias anyway."

"Just be glad you're alive." The chief's voice softened. "Thanks for the help. Now go home and rest."

"You know I can't rest yet," she protested, "and don't I deserve to be kept in the loop?"

Silence. Then Houghton sighed. "As long as you stay safe. If you take even the tiniest risk, I'll throw you in jail too."

"I'll behave. Being a prisoner for one night was one night too long."

The chief said, "Let me talk to Jackson."

She passed the phone to him.

After Jackson had shared a few details about their location, they hurried back. Jackson remained on guard at the cave's mouth.

As expected, Sadie still had things well in hand.

Liz sat beside her and slipped an arm around Lydia.

Sadie said, "I thought we'd be skipping through heaven together by now. A little disappointing, in a way."

"We'll do it someday, friend." Liz patted Sadie's free arm. "But we still have work to do here."

Lydia nestled in Liz's arms like a weary little bird. Finally, she raised her head. "My *Bubby*. I must go home to Addie. And Dale."

"I'll take you," Sadie offered, "but we'll have to hike back to my Jeep." Her grin returned as she glanced sideways at Liz. "You've got unfinished business, right?"

Liz nodded. "I'll catch a ride with Jackson or Houghton."

The mayor called from his post, "Kristen still tied up?"

"I double-checked the knots," Sadie answered.

"I don't think she's going anywhere. No reason for you to have to stay in there."

Sadie pulled on Liz's arm. "Come on. We are *so* outta this cave!"

Lydia jumped up with sudden energy. Behind the others, Liz burst through its mouth into the brilliant August sunlight she had ignored earlier, consumed with calling the chief.

Now, basking in warmth and radiance, Liz recalled last week's sermon. *Is this how Lazarus felt?*

Jackson offered them his backpack, full of bottles of water and muffins Naomi had sent. "She knew we'd find you, safe and sound."

Mmm. Liz munched one, loving her friend's faith even more than the fabulous taste.

Jackson continued to scan the forest, holding the gun ready. "The chief's okayed Lydia and Sadie to go home after he arrives. His officers will take Kristen in." He turned to Liz. "The chief said you and I can ride with him to the Fort Wayne police station—if you want."

"I want." Liz's thoughts shifted from their survival to Cyrus's. Without Kristen's presence, could Tyler rise above greed enough to let his grandfather live?

She took a second muffin and a bottle of water, then walked toward the cave.

Sadie stared. "Hey, why're you going back in there?"

"Kristen might be hungry." Liz ducked back into the cave's twilight to the huddled form by the wall, head bowed to her chest. Kristen didn't look up.

Liz slipped her gag from her mouth, then jumped back, not really surprised when Kristen spat at her and swore. She waited until her enemy temporarily ran out of vocabulary and spit. *If you weren't dry before, you are now.* "Want a drink?"

The woman's eyes widened, then narrowed. Finally, she nodded.

Liz held the bottle to her lips, and Kristen gulped.

She held the muffin up, and the woman ate.

Liz didn't expect thanks, and she didn't receive any. When Kristen was done eating, Liz replaced the gag, narrowly avoiding being bitten. Kristen's glare followed her to the cave's mouth.

Lydia stared, her jaw slack, as Liz reemerged.

Sadie rolled her eyes. "You're crazy, Liz."

Jackson gave her a quizzical glance. "Glad to see you're still alive."

Liz smiled. "Me too." Suddenly she realized she hadn't combed her hair. She glanced at her filthy shorts and shirt. She did indeed look—and probably smelled—as if she'd just crawled out of a cave.

Jackson read her mind. "Don't worry about it. No one expects you to be forcibly held overnight in a cave and come out looking like a movie star."

She wet a corner of her shirt and was dabbing at her face when Chief Houghton and Officers Dixon, Herst, and Hughes appeared.

For once, the crusty chief abandoned professional reserve and threw his arms around Liz. "I know I should probably scold you, but I'm so happy to see you. I'm sure you've learned your lesson."

Liz raised an eyebrow, her lips curling mischievously.

The chief chuckled. "You're right. I forgot who I was talking to for a second there." He ordered Herst and Hughes to retrieve Kristen from the cave.

While they fetched and handcuffed her, Houghton asked Liz if she still wanted to go with them. "No time for breaks on the way out, I'm afraid. We have to move, then reach Fort Wayne as fast as we can."

"I'm good." With Naomi's muffins, her sharpness had returned.

Houghton told Dixon to accompany Lydia and Sadie back to her Jeep. "With those other two perps on the loose, we can't be too cautious."

Liz hugged her friends good-bye.

Sadie waggled a finger at her. "Stay out of trouble, you hear?"

"Always," Liz deadpanned, then matched their grins, the first they'd shared in what seemed forever.

Adrenaline flowing through her veins, Liz kept up with the chief and Jackson as they walked to the Boy Scout camp, where the police car was parked.

By hike's end, her legs had gone limp, and she thought she'd fall dead asleep in the police car's backseat. Its siren kept her awake, though, as they zoomed over country roads and interstates at scenery-blurring speeds.

As Houghton drove, Jackson relayed information from his officers. Kristen's fingerprints matched those of a Kristen Baker, though she sometimes used the surname Wilson.

Jackson's face darkened as he hung up. "Dixon said they found Harvey in one of the smaller caves in that patch of woods. Coroner says he was stabbed to death last night."

Liz dropped back against the seat, horror wringing her from head to toe. Poor, foolish man, whose sins did not begin to compare to those of his murderers. She choked, "Why did he ever get mixed up with those—those—"

"The usual story," Jackson said sadly. "Money. Harvey's store wasn't doing well. He was probably desperate to pay his property taxes that had stacked up for several years. That information's public, and I'll bet Kristen and Ty used it to trap him." Jackson turned and reached for Liz's hand. Without a word, she squeezed his, her mind painting ghastly pictures of what had happened and what might have been.

Jackson answered the chief's phone again. He hung up, his voice terse. "They've tracked down Cyrus's bank and are on their way." He looked up the location on his phone and directed Houghton.

Liz winced as the police car careened through traffic. *This reminds me way too much of riding behind Sadie on her motorcycle.* But she leaned forward, resting her arms on the front seat, glad for no separating screen so she wouldn't miss a thing.

"This might be the right bank," Houghton commented dryly as his police car joined several others surrounding the limestone building.

"Keep her safe," he barked to Jackson, then dashed to join other uniformed officers.

Liz watched helmeted policemen wearing vests labeled SWAT in clean white letters. A man with a bullhorn ordered Ty to give himself up. As officers scattered, Liz's pulse thudded so she could barely hear Jackson's voice.

"These guys know their stuff. They'll get Cyrus out of there." He covered her hand with his.

Words strangled each other in her throat.

She wanted the old man safe, but she didn't want anyone shot—not even Ty. Why did people *do* these things? Why couldn't they all live in peace and help each other instead of stealing and killing?

"I know." Jackson seemed to have read her mind. He encircled her with his strong arm. "I know, Liz."

At that moment, Ty and Mr. Whittington, faces white as chalk, exited the bank's front door, hands raised above their heads. Officers swarmed in, handcuffed Ty, and hurried him off to a police car. Houghton and another policeman clasped his grandfather on either side and walked him away.

Liz, with Jackson on her heels, exited the police car and dashed for her friend. She threw her arms around Mr. Whittington, who returned her embrace, saying, "Oh, Liz, thank God you're all right."

22

Oh, the ecstasy of a good night's sleep on a soft, clean bed, without people waving guns at her.

Liz wiggled her toes in the sheets, luxuriating in the sunlight that greeted her this safe, beautiful morning.

She hoped Mr. Whittington, recuperating from dehydration and exposure in a Fort Wayne hospital, felt safe too. After his grandson's betrayal, the old gentleman's recovery would take a while. Still, she hoped to cheer him with a visit this afternoon. After he was released from the hospital, she and the Material Girls would nurse him back to health.

Until then, with no guests due until tomorrow afternoon, Liz planned a leisurely day of reading and eating the Danish pastries Naomi had left. Having heard of the crisis, Naomi had taken Beans to her house. Last night, notified of the rescues, Naomi brought the pastries and tacked up a banner that read, *Welcome home, Liz!*

Beans is fine. I'll keep him as long as you like, she'd written on a note stuck to the pastry box. *Sleep till noon! Sleep three days in a row! You deserve it!*

Liz glanced at her bedside clock. Not yet noon, but close to it. She rose, brewed hazelnut coffee, then devoured a cheese Danish and a ripe peach for lunch. Then she took a long, blissful shower.

Afterward, her fingers itched to call Chief Houghton. Was Ty indeed Sherry's son? Had the police found Cyrus's tea set yet?

After an hour of mental ping-pong, she called him.

"You just can't leave it alone, can you?"

The chief's words, a repeat of Ty's, shocked her to silence. Then she recognized his teasing tone and laughed. "You knew I'd call."

"Of course I did. Sorry, but neither perp has talked much, so I don't have much to report. We did find out that Tyler's last name is Johnson. He is definitely Cyrus's grandson."

So he was Sherry's son. How sad.

"Whittington said he and Tyler had a falling out after the boy flunked out of college. Wanted his grandpa to hand over money so Tyler could have his own acting company. When Whittington told him he'd have to work for his dreams like everybody else, Tyler didn't take it well."

"I think that's an understatement. What about the missing tea set?"

She could imagine Houghton's head-scratching just by his tone as he said, "When we started talking plea bargain, both admitted to trashing Lydia's and Dale's house. They wanted to find her tea set—which, by the way, she does own—and destroy any tangible proof she was kin to Whittington, thinking that would hurt her claim as heir to his fortune. But neither Tyler nor Kristen has confessed to stealing Whittington's tea set. There were too many people around the inn to pull it off, they said."

"They could have saved a lot of time and trouble by just obtaining a DNA test to see if Cyrus and Lydia were related," Liz said, "though, of course, Lydia never would have consented to one. They'd have had to do it on the sly. Still, they might not be facing kidnapping and murder charges if they'd used their brains."

"Yep," the chief agreed, "but greedy people with an ax to grind often forget to."

She thanked him and hung up. Some blanks had been filled, but she still had questions. She was drooping, and her stomach wasn't handling the Danish well. It occurred to her that maybe she shouldn't have consumed something that rich when she'd eaten so little in the past twenty-four hours. *A kick in the stomach probably didn't help matters.*

She plopped onto the sitting room sofa with a novel, then awoke two hours later, drooling slightly on the book.

Maybe she did need to sleep for three days straight.

She'd just finished combing her hair out of her eyes when the doorbell rang.

She hoped it was just a delivery person. At least she'd gotten a good nap. Liz hurried out into the rotunda and opened the front door.

"Well, it's about time. You've got this place locked up like Alcatraz."

The Brumpett sisters.

Fortunately—or not so fortunately—Sarah had readied the Rose of Sharon Room for guests. Maxine, spouting wrathful diatribes against their Michigan relatives, moved back in with a delight that escalated Liz's headache. Marlene said very little. Maybe today she really was sick.

Houghton dropped by briefly to see how Liz was, and, predictably, Maxine exploded.

"The police! Again?"

Marlene wrung her hands and whimpered.

After the chief left, Liz frankly summarized Cyrus's situation for the sisters. Perhaps her SWAT team saga would scare off the Brumpetts.

Despite Maxine's escalating displeasure, she said she would stay because the Rose of Sharon Room had become home to her—a line that scared Liz *almost* as much as what she'd just been through in the cave.

Marlene, however, disagreed. "I don't want to stay here, Maxine. This place frightens me."

Maxine brushed off her objection as if she were a fly. "Don't be ridiculous."

Instead of caving or manipulating, Marlene raised her voice. "I will not remain here even one night, Maxine. Let's go."

"We are *not* leaving," Maxine bellowed. "Discussion over."

Marlene screeched, "Yes, the discussion's over because I am packing now. No matter what you say!"

She stomped up the stairs with a firmness that belied her earlier back disabilities. Maxine stormed off to sulk in the four-season room.

Liz recklessly finished off the cheese Danish.

Hearing smothered sobs as she carried towels upstairs, Liz longed to escape to her apartment. But the quavering pain in Marlene's voice couldn't be ignored.

Liz tapped on the door. There was no answer. The indignant mother in her insisted on knowing if Maxine was torturing her sister, so she opened it a crack.

Marlene was packing, all right. In her hands, she held cute little velvet pincushions.

Liz's pincushions. The unique ones she'd purchased at Hamminger House in Kokomo.

She swung the door open. "Marlene, what are you doing? Those are mine."

The woman's eyes widened like a child's, and she clutched them to her chest. "No they aren't."

"Yes they are." Liz entered, her hand outstretched. "Please give them to me."

In answer, Marlene held them behind her back, her lip stuck out.

"What's going on here?" Maxine barged in. Her face whitened, and her hands dropped to her side. She murmured, "Marlene—"

"No. I want them. They're pretty."

Maxine's face crumpled. "I'm so sorry, Liz. I thought she was over this."

Maxine strode to Marlene's oversized suitcase and, with her sister whining and sobbing at her elbow, tore out its contents.

Among the tangle of clothes, Liz saw an assortment of odd objects. A fake Hawaiian lei. A wooden plaque with a barometer on it. A child's bent Slinky. A lovely music box in the shape of a heart.

Maxine swore under her breath. Marlene bawled.

Her sister yanked out a bottle of furniture polish, then half-used skeins of embroidery floss and needles. Liz's breath caught in her throat. Hadn't Sarah and Sadie mentioned missing those very things?

Liz's stained glass refrigerator magnet and the white marble bunny she thought she'd put away with the Easter decorations appeared, followed by Mr. Whittington's canning jars.

Maxine's next discovery was the ugliest glass elephant Liz had ever seen.

From the bottom of the suitcase, Maxine pulled out an elegant black case, bound with a satin elastic band. "Marlene, you didn't!" she gasped. She opened it and gaped at the tea set, with its lavender, purple, and yellow butterflies looking as if they had just landed on the teapot, cups, sugar bowl, and creamer. "This belonged to Cyrus's daughter! How could you?"

"I knew you would take them away!" Marlene wailed. She threw herself on the bed.

Maxine's face quivered, tears gathering in her eyes as she met Liz's gaze. "Please, Liz, don't have her arrested. I'll get her more help. I promise."

———— //////////////////// ————

Jackson sat in the hospital waiting room with Liz and listened as she told him about the Brumpetts. At story's end, he simply stared.

"Not exactly what I deduced," Liz said dryly. "Marlene sneaked it out of Mr. Whittington's room while Sarah was in and out, cleaning. At least Chief Houghton didn't really consider an inside job either." She couldn't keep back a chuckle. "Neither of us could have begun to imagine this scenario."

"Who would? It's just lucky that they came back for you to bust them."

"I won't prosecute, and neither will Mr. Whittington. Marlene is quite ill." Liz sighed, remembering Maxine's broken apologies for Marlene's kleptomania, her desperate hope that her sister could be cured.

"At any rate, he'll get his treasured tea set back." She stroked the satin band, the elegant brocaded surface of the box. "I hope this will speed his healing."

Jackson looked at his watch. "Think his doctor's gone by now?"

"We can check." She stood.

Jackson carried the box as they walked side by side down the hall. He waited outside the door while Liz entered.

She froze in the doorway.

Along with his top hat, Mr. Whittington wore an old-fashioned nightshirt that could have graced Ebenezer Scrooge in *A Christmas Carol*.

Except that it was covered with big polka dots. Red, yellow, and blue polka dots.

"Hullo, sweet Liz," the patient beamed, extending his arms. "Do you like my hospital attire? Sadie found it for me when I told her how utterly boring their nightshirts were."

She hugged him and laughed, but her laughter soon turned to tears. How could she ever have suspected this sweet man of being anything sinister? And how close she had come to losing him!

"Dear child, I didn't mean to upset you." He drew back, wiping her tears with his paisley handkerchief.

"I'm fine. More than fine." She sniffled, then chuckled again, partially at being called "child" at forty years of age. "I am glad to see you doing so well."

His hands still shook, but his pale face had pinked a little. And his sparkle was certainly returning. "The doctor says I might go home tomorrow. My house is almost ready. But . . . would you mind if I come and spend a bit more time at your inn? I'll try not to be a bother."

She clucked her tongue at his hesitation. "Of course you may come. I'll talk to your nurse about the logistics."

His face broke into a smile the size of Big Ben, and his own eyes watered. "How lovely." He covered his mouth with a conspirator's gesture. "They're very nice here, but I can hardly wait to eat food that tastes like food."

Laughing again, she gestured to Jackson, who carried in the box.

Mr. Whittington's mouth formed an *O*, his eyes sparkling like giant sapphires. "Is it—can it be—?"

"It's your tea set." Liz removed the lid. "Would you care for a cuppa?"

23

I cannot believe you talked me into this again." Opal aimed a half-hearted glare at Sadie as they arranged sleeping bags on the table bed in Sadie's camper.

"I should hang out in caves with homicidal maniacs more often," Sadie countered, "so you'll appreciate me the way you should."

Arranging hers on one of the real beds, Liz grinned. She'd only achieved this better bed status because Opal flatly refused to sleep on either end.

"I don't care how many times you've checked the supports," she insisted, "never again, Sadie Schwarzentruber. *Never.*"

"You just want to be close to me," Sadie teased.

Opal *harrumphed* and rolled her eyes heavenward.

Liz hadn't anticipated a return to a campground within the next decade either, especially with the inn's air-conditioning working so well.

Since surviving their ordeal, however, Sadie had plugged endlessly for a big-time celebration, especially during quilting sessions.

"The good guys won! The bad guys are in jail!" she chortled, prancing around the workroom. "We should *par-tee*!"

When they all agreed, she informed them she'd already made the campsite reservation.

Opposition arose, polite and not so polite.

But Sadie won.

Maybe because she'd hung blown-up photos of s'mores cakes all over the workroom. Or maybe because she was actually right. They needed to talk out what had happened. And they needed to celebrate their happy ending.

The weather had cooperated as if programmed for a campout.

"Zero chance of rain, upper seventies at the highest." Mary Ann had been monitoring reports religiously.

While they set up camp, Beans had made himself at home directly in front of the door.

The Material Girls swam in the still-warm lake and hiked the beautiful trails.

"Lots more fun than the last time we hiked," Liz told Sadie.

"You can say that again."

As they gathered around Naomi's fire, Liz saw a top hat coming around the road's curve. She dashed out to meet Mr. Whittington. "You're just in time!"

He wore camo cargo pants for the occasion, accented by a mauve dress shirt and plaid slippers. He swept off his hat and made a deep bow. "How kind of you ladies to have invited me to join you for this illustrious occasion."

"So glad you could come, Cyrus." Sadie hugged him.

"Hey, you won't be the only guy," Caitlyn spoke up. "Eric's off duty tonight. He's coming too."

She and the park ranger had discovered even more in common than camper supports.

"George is coming for dessert." Opal dimpled.

Her husband of fifty-plus years talked maybe once a month, but Opal still lit up when he was around.

Why did hot dogs taste a hundred times better around a campfire than anywhere else? Liz slathered her half-charred wonder with ketchup and dill pickles.

Sadie, Naomi, Mr. Whittington, and Eric were brave enough to add Sadie's homemade "atomic sauce." Eric, gulping water by the quart, pronounced it delicious.

The sky erupted in carnival colors as the sun set. Stars swam in the innocent deep blue sky like schools of tiny glowing fish. Liz almost wished they wouldn't talk about the ordeal they'd endured. But that comprised part of the celebration. Mr. Whittington especially needed to talk about it. Plus, some who didn't know details wanted to hear his story. That was how she and Sadie had persuaded him to open up.

So now the group quieted as the old gentleman began, "I suppose it all began with a love story."

"We like those." Mary Ann encouraged him with a smile, and the others murmured assent.

He filled in the group about his family history, about his father and Sally and little Priscilla. About how James never saw them again. About the letters in which Mr. Whittington discovered the truth about his family.

"My parents, wife, and only daughter having passed away, this discovery brightened my life. I was determined to find Priscilla."

"I would have done the same thing." Opal gave a decided nod. "Family is family."

"Unfortunately, my college-aged grandson stole the letters." The old gentleman's mouth tightened. "Until then, he had been my sole heir, the son of my only daughter, Sherry, who died young, shortly after giving birth to Tyler actually. I loved Tyler. My wife and I raised him. I love him still. But we have never gotten along."

That everyone knew, thanks to extensive media coverage of the bank standoff. A murmur of sympathy ran through the group.

"Marilyn and I did our best, but he grew up bitter because of Sherry's death and his father's desertion. Tyler was talented, but he failed at three different colleges. When he demanded I fully fund his acting company, I told him I would not help until he learned to apply himself. All his life, Tyler has counted on my leaving my estate to him.

"Thanks to my father's canny business sense and God's blessings, my glassworks prospered amazingly. But I prefer a simple lifestyle. I have arranged my affairs so that my name is not known. I like it that way."

He'd certainly accomplished that goal. Though he was a millionaire, Liz hadn't been able to find his name on the Internet.

"Tyler saw wealth the wrong way." Mr. Whittington shook his head. "When he found evidence that other heirs might share in my estate, he became determined they would not. Unfortunately, he began dating Kristen Baker, whom he'd met in theater classes at school.

"She was without conscience." His eyes sparked. "Kristen helped Ty find Sally's niece, Lois Hershberger. Lois had adored her aunt Sally and had visited her, her husband, Solomon, and daughter, Priscilla, in Indiana several times. She occasionally visited Priscilla as they both grew old."

Liz hadn't heard this part of the story. "Ty didn't tell you?"

"No. I had found Lois as well, but she followed her Amish family's tenets and refused to tell me anything. Ty and Kristen, however, threatened her into revealing where Priscilla's family was. That is why they came to Indiana shortly before I did, one step ahead of me."

"But you found Lydia before they did!" Sadie pointed out.

"Actually, Ty suspected our kinship first." Mr. Whittington's eyes flashed. "Enough to tear Lydia's house apart, seeking the tea set so he could destroy evidence we were related.

"He and Kristen used every means they could think of—including loosening Sadie's camper supports—to frighten Liz so she would not help me in my quest. But they underestimated her."

He beamed at Liz, only to lower his head as he reddened. "Not that I was lily-white in my pursuit of family. I secretly followed Liz almost as much as Tyler and Kristen did, which must have been nerve-racking, to say the least. She did research at the courthouse that bore fruit, whereas I manipulated a nosy courthouse clerk into telling me about it."

Liz laughed, inviting the rest to laugh with her. Mr. Whittington was an operator, all right. A lonely one—whom she hoped would be lonely no more.

"How did Tyler and Kristen know about that woods near the Boy Scout camp?" Naomi asked.

Mr. Whittington grimaced. "I sent Tyler to that Boy Scout camp when he was younger because of my fond childhood memories of Indiana. I hoped he would learn woodcraft and some of the moral values the Scouts promote." He sighed. "One of two is not a very good average. Nothing I did seemed to work."

"Parents and grandparents can only do their best," Mary Ann said kindly, but firmly. "You must live your life in the present, Cyrus."

His face brightened. "And I have much for which to give thanks. Lydia came to see me this past week. She even let me meet Addie."

Liz and the others cheered.

"Did you invite her here tonight?" Opal asked.

"I did." He sobered. "However, her husband—for very good reasons—is quite wary of me. But the important thing is that we have connected." His smile shone bright and warm as the fire. "Perhaps the next time we gather, Lydia will see fit to come—"

"Next time?" a young voice interrupted. "Then perhaps I should go home?"

The old gentleman started. "Lydia!"

His eyes sparkled as she strode forward and clasped his hands. The night rang with laughter and good wishes.

Jackson, who had brought Lydia, stood beside Liz. "How did she talk Dale into this?" he whispered.

"She's small, but mighty," Liz recalled Lydia's fiery phone call. "I imagine when she makes up her mind, he realizes he'd better consider her viewpoint."

"But she was dead set against meeting Cyrus, wasn't she?"

"She was scared, recovering after a burglary, remember? For all she knew at the time, he was involved."

Lydia had walked to the picnic table and opened a box she had placed there. She turned to the group. "My Grossmutter Eunice, whom I loved dearly, gave me her Mutter Priscilla's set before she passed away." Her voice quavered for moment, then steadied as she smiled. "Would you all like to see it?"

Caitlyn, Eric, and Naomi shone flashlights on the lovely tea set—whereupon Cyrus brought out *his* set to more oohs and ahhs. Sadie lit a propane lantern and held it high, illuminating the table as if indoors.

James had created similar sets for his daughter and granddaughter, both floral patterns accented with butterflies. But he'd designed smaller butterflies for his daughter's set, grouping them here and there. He'd painted tiny pink tulips on Lydia's, whereas he'd used bigger, single butterflies and miniscule yellow roses on Mr. Whittington's.

Both are exquisite—similar, yet so different. Liz ran her finger along the china's gilt edges. Who would ever have imagined these two sets—and these two people—would appear side by side?

"Do you suppose," Mr. Whittington flashed his unforgettable smile at Lydia, "we could have the tea party of the century here at the campground? If everyone is *very* careful, of course."

"It is a special occasion." Lydia's head bobbed in agreement. Her smile almost matched his, and for a moment the family resemblance was striking.

Naomi heated the coffee she'd brought, water for tea, and two containers of fudge sauce on the fire's grill.

"Time to break out the marshmallows!" Caitlyn opened a giant bag. "I need at least forty golden brown ones for two s'mores cakes."

Eager to comply, the group produced them in record time while Liz helped Lydia and Cyrus set up their dishes on the picnic table. Caitlyn poured fudge on the cakes and lavished marshmallows on top.

"I haven't been to a tea party since my cousin's when we were four," Eric, the off-duty ranger, cradled a small rosebud cup in his big hands after wolfing s'mores cake from a paper plate. "I don't remember it being quite like this one."

"My friends are unique." Caitlyn sipped demurely from her pink tulip cup, pinky extended.

Jackson had promised to take Lydia home after the party, she knew, but sitting with him later by the fire was beyond pleasant. Liz sighed.

"I really hate to go," he whispered, "but this is, after all, a girl thing. Will you have dinner with me next weekend? We could celebrate your survival all over again."

"And your rescue skills." She smiled, then helped gather Lydia's dishes back into the box.

Cyrus collected his too. "Time to return to my house. It's very nice to have my own space again. But I should love to visit Pleasant Creek soon. Reg is simply dying to take a drive or two or three in the countryside."

"I can do that," Sadie said, and the other Material Girls offered to help Reg out too.

Sadie and Cyrus, Caitlyn and Eric, and Opal and George walked to the parking lot to say their good-byes, making Liz miss Jackson all the more.

But she, Mary Ann, and Naomi savored the tranquil night together after all the brouhaha.

"Always quieter when Sadie's gone." A wicked grin crossed Mary Ann's face.

"A little peace and quiet doesn't hurt," Naomi agreed. "Liz, do you know if Lydia has come to grips with Cyrus's fortune? After all, it's not every day someone wants to make you a millionaire."

"She doesn't say much about it." Liz poked the fire. "But Cyrus told me she's begun to consider the possibility of being his heir if she could funnel most of the money into, say, improving medical facilities in Pleasant Creek so we—and especially the Amish—don't have to travel to bigger towns for care."

"That would be wonderful," Mary Ann enthused. "I hope she goes through with it."

Liz and her friends listened to the crackling of the fire and felt its warmth on their faces, content to be together. A few minutes later Sadie, Opal, and Caitlyn returned and sat down, and their group was complete again. Naomi stuck another marshmallow on a stick and held it over the fire. "Liz, didn't you suspect that appliance salesman who showed up at the same time Cyrus did?"

Liz chuckled ruefully. "Poor Tony Lanham. Yes, at one time, I thought he might have been stealing valuables like expensive glass. I had no idea Tony had been let go by his impossible boss near the end of his conference."

"That nice young man?" Mary Ann frowned. "He seemed like the hardworking type."

"He probably is. But when I tried to contact Tony, he was so depressed he didn't answer his phone or email. In a panic at losing his job, he moved out of his apartment and back to his parents' house. His former workplace only told me they employed no one by that name—not that they'd laid him off. So I was left thinking he'd lied about everything and had stolen the tea set, especially when he turned up unexpectedly at my inn at exactly the time it was taken."

"That would do it," Naomi said. "But I assume you found out different?"

"Oh, yes. Soon after Cyrus was rescued, Tony called me back, excited that he'd been hired by a new company." Liz laughed, shaking her head. "When he'd abruptly showed up, then left before I came back from the campout, he'd returned to our area to interview for this sudden job opening. Oh, and Sadie? I think I know why Beans loved him so much."

"Why?" Sadie demanded, giving away her persistent dislike for the man who'd asked to buy her beloved bulldog.

"Tony mentioned that he keeps a bacon-scented air freshener in his car. The scent probably stays on him."

A broad grin broke over Sadie's face. "Ha! I knew our Beansy wouldn't leave us."

Beans whuffled and flopped his head down on Sadie's foot.

"A happy ending." Mary Ann smiled. "Love it."

"Me too." Liz poked the fire, her inner glow answering its warmth. She'd hoped against hope that Tony was innocent and was relieved to know that he was.

Naomi held up a finger. "One more question: What will happen to those Rumschpringe boys who tore up each other's barns? They aren't going to put the whole bunch in jail, are they?"

"No, the chief told me that Gideon Sommer probably will be the only one who does substantial jail time," Liz answered. "The others are first-time offenders. Apparently, the judge in the case is listening to the bishop and the boys' families, who promise they will work until they've paid for every cent of the damage they caused. At most, he'll sentence them to a weekend or two in jail."

"Just enough to scare some sense into them," Mary Ann said, "though I imagine their 'hard labor' sentences will convince them even better."

"Did we scare off Eric tonight?" Mary Ann teased Caitlyn.

"You underestimate me." Caitlyn flipped her hair in a movie-star gesture.

They finally headed to bed, stepping over Beans, for whom the evening had simply been too much.

I hope you'll be too tired to protect us from lethal raccoons tonight.

Liz crawled into her sleeping bag. Naomi luxuriated in open windows on all sides of their bed.

But Sadie and Opal, lying on the table-bed, could not seem to settle.

"Your feet are cold," Sadie complained.

"Not as cold as yours," Opal retorted. "George's are nice and warm."

"Move over."

"*You* move over."

"But I'm the grand champion apron seamstress of the world."

"You may have the ribbon, but you know perfectly well my apron was better than yours—"

As the apron warriors duked it out, Liz buried her head under her pillow and smiled.

It was nice to know that things were definitely back to normal.

Learn more about Annie's fiction books at

AnniesFiction.com

- Access your e-books
- Discover exciting new series
- Read sample chapters
- Watch video book trailers
- Share your feedback

We've designed the Annie's Fiction website especially for you!

Plus, manage your account online!

- Check your account status
- Make payments online
- Update your address

Visit us at AnniesFiction.com